THE MULLIGAN CHRONICLES

Talking Dog $20

Doghouse Edition

by Martin Thompson

Cowtown Publishing · Fort Worth, Texas

Copyright © 2026 Martin Thompson. All rights reserved.
No part of this book may be reproduced, stored in a retrieval system, or transmitted in any form or by any means—electronic, mechanical, photocopying, recording, or otherwise—without the prior written permission of the author, except for brief quotations used in reviews or other noncommercial uses permitted by copyright law.

This is a work of fiction. Names, characters, places, and incidents are either the product of the author's imagination or are used fictitiously. Any resemblance to actual persons, living or dead, or to actual events is purely coincidental.

ISBN 979-8-9944181-5-4 (paperback)
ISBN 979-8-9944181-4-7 (hardcover)
ISBN 979-8-9944181-6-1 (ebook)
Published in 2026 by Cowtown Publishing
Fort Worth, Texas
Printed in the United States of America

Dedication

For Janice,
my partner in every good story.

Every dog I have ever had the privilege to love and love me back

And for anyone who has ever loved a pet
and quietly agreed to let them run the world—
this book is yours.

Author's Note

Sometimes a story doesn't arrive quietly.

Sometimes it kicks down the door, tells a joke, and demands a snack.

That's how Mulligan first showed up for me.

When I wrote Talking Dog $20, I let my imagination run free. Mulligan told bigger and bigger stories — about shadowy criminals, famous friends, unlikely heroes, and ridiculous adventures that stretched well past the edge of believability. It was fun. It was outrageous. And I loved every minute of it.

That book was written in laughter.

But here's the funny thing about stories — especially the good ones.

Sometimes the lies you tell for fun turn out to be truths wearing costumes.

In the end, even Mulligan's wildest exaggerations seemed to carry a kind of strange honesty. The people he invented showed up. The impossible began to feel oddly… possible. And what started as a joke slowly revealed something deeper beneath the surface.

This book is still exactly what it pretends to be — a tall tale about a talking dog. But it's also a celebration of imagination, hope, and the idea that sometimes the world needs a little nonsense in order to survive the serious parts.

If you later meet Mulligan again in another version of this story, you may find him softer, wiser, and a little more grounded.

That doesn't mean this one was wrong.

It just means he had more to say.

— Martin Thompson

Preface

For nearly fifty years, I've stood beside families at some of their most difficult moments. I've watched grief enter rooms quietly and leave them changed. I've also learned that even in the heaviest hours, laughter has a way of sneaking in—often when it's least expected and most needed.

This story grew out of that space.

Talking Dog $20 is about second chances—some earned, some accidental, and some delivered with a wagging tail and a list of demands. It's about the strange grace that shows up when life stops making sense and insists on being lived anyway. Along the way, it touches on faith, friendship, marriage, memory, and the peculiar ways love insists on rearranging our plans.

At its heart, this is a story about listening—listening to people, to silence, and sometimes to voices we'd rather dismiss as impossible. Because every once in a while, the thing that sounds the most unbelievable is the very thing we need to hear.

If this book makes you laugh, I'm glad.
If it makes you pause, I'm grateful.
And if it reminds you of someone—human or otherwise—who changed your life simply by showing up, then it has done its job.

— **Martin Thompson**
Fort Worth, Texas

Table of Contents

Contents

Author's Note iii

Preface iv

Table of Contents v

Chapter 1 — Talking Dog $20 2

Chapter 2 — Mulligan's First Bath 6

Chapter 3 — Mulligan Makes His Stand 12

Chapter 4 — Shopping List for a Canine Diva 18

Chapter 5 — Appraisals, Purchases, and a Runway Dog 24

Chapter 6 — Back-Seat Nuptials 30

Chapter 7 — Two at a Time 36

Chapter 8 — The Re-Introduction 42

Chapter 9 — Contract Negotiations 50

Chapter 10 — Of Rabbis, Priests & Dog Ball Ejectors 56

Chapter 11 — Bonjour, Agent Canin Spécial 62

Chapter 12 — Dinner Is Served (and So Are the Demands) 68

Chapter 13 — A Priest, a Rabbi, and a Talking Dog Walk into a Church 74

Chapter 14 — Dominoes, Doubts, and Dog Tales 82

Chapter 15 — Movie Night and Lime Etiquette 90

Chapter 16 — Mulligan the Multilingual Miracle 96

Chapter 17 — Floral Budgets and Other Miracles 106

Chapter 18 — The Table Knows 112

Chapter 19 — The Chef, the Casket, and the Confession 120

Chapter 20 — Gold on Gold (and a Chef) 128

Chapter 21 — Sidecar Diplomacy 136

Chapter 22 — The Doctor, the Diet, and the Dying Appetite 144

Chapter 23 — The Italian Invasion 150

Chapter 24 — Lunch, Language, and Light Sarcasm 158

Chapter 25 — Signora Bella (and the Swiffer) 164

Chapter 26 — Everest, Eleven Doves, and a Swiffer 174

Chapter 27 — Renovations, Revelations, and a Remarkable Invoice 184

Chapter 28 — Bulletins, Beards, and a Beagle Choir 190

Chapter 29 — Hors d'Oeuvres, Code Names, and a Very Specific Blessing 198

Chapter 30 — Steam, Brass, and Lemon-Linen 206

Chapter 31 — Vest, Gin, and Rug-Beating 216

Chapter 32 — Knuckles, Blanks, and the Medal of Deniability .. 220

Chapter 33 — The Rooms of Miracles (and Mild Panic) 228

Chapter 34 — The Funeral of the Century 236

Chapter 35 — Something Borrowed, Something Blue (and Ten Sky-Trackers) 244

Chapter 36 — Doors Lights Breath 252

Chapter 37 — The Morning After 262

Chapter 38 — The Best Decision I Ever Made 270

Acknowledgments 276

About the Author 277

Chapter 1 — Talking Dog $20

One afternoon, I was driving back from a graveside service, still thinking about the flower easel that had toppled over and the woman who stepped into a fire-ant bed and looked like she was performing an exorcism, when a hand-painted sign nailed to a crooked post made me tap the brakes:

TALKING DOG — $20

I'd seen my share of odd things, but that one stopped me. At first, I told myself it had to be a gimmick. Keep driving. Move along. But curiosity got better of me, so I pulled over and walked up the path.

A fellow in a stained T-shirt answered the door like this sort of thing happened all the time.

"I'm here about the talking dog," I said.

"Come on in," he replied.

He called out, "Mulligan!" and the dog trotted in—scruffy, tail wagging, hair doing its best to defy gravity—looking like he'd just rolled out of a bunker at Colonial. The man nodded toward the couch.

"Go on," he said. "Do your thing."

Mulligan hopped up, sat square, and looked me straight in the eye.

"Hi," he said, plain as you please. "I'm Mulligan, and I'm a talking dog."

I nearly fell off the couch. A talking dog named Mulligan. For a man who measures life in guest books and floral sprays, this was a lot to take in—especially from a dog with a golf name. I loved it.

"What's your story?" I asked.

Mulligan didn't hesitate. He launched into it like he'd been rehearsing for this very moment.

"When I was a pup," he said, "I belonged to a drug lord named Jefe. Jefe figured out pretty quickly what I could do. I'd sit in rooms and listen, then tell him who was stealing his stuff, who was skimming, and who might be thinking about putting a hit on him."

He paused, as if gauging my reaction.

"One day, a supermodel Afghan hound named Farah came trotting by, and I fell in love. We got married and started having puppies. With my good looks and Farah's supermodel looks, the puppies were magnificent. People paid fifteen grand for them."

I stayed quiet.

"Well," he continued, "Farah got nervous about my work for Jefe and asked me to find something safer. I worked for the police, then the FBI, and finally the CIA. Helped solve a lot of crimes. Even thwarted a major terrorist plot."

Naturally.

"After that," Mulligan said, "Farah asked me to find something safer again. So I became a dog trainer. I can teach a dog in days what it takes humans months to learn. I speak dog and human. That's my gift."

He sat back, satisfied.

"So," he said, "that's my story."

He told it with the confident delivery of someone who knew exactly how tall to make his tales—names dropped, impossible details tossed in, just enough bravado to make nonsense sound official.

I turned to the owner. "Why are you selling this dog for twenty dollars?"

The man shrugged. "Because he's a liar. He made every bit of that up."

That should have been the end of it. But Mulligan had a presence you couldn't quite put down—the kind that makes people set their coffee aside and lean in.

For twenty dollars, I pictured a dog steady at a graveside, calm through a visitation, and ridiculous in all the right ways. I heard the absurdity of it, and I liked it.

"All right," I said, before I could talk myself out of it. "I'll take him."

"Sure, you will," the man said, like he'd seen worse.

He handed me a crumpled bag of dog biscuits for parting advice, and Mulligan leapt into the passenger seat like he'd been born there. He smelled of outdoors and old stories. His fur stuck up in places that suggested a life lived in motion.

As I drove away, Mulligan's monologue kept running through my head—Jefe, Farah, FBI—and I found myself smiling. I told myself I'd clean him up, take him to a groomer, and then figure out how to tell Julia.

That's how most good misadventures begin: with a crooked sign, a couch, and a dog who insists on telling his life like a country song.

I didn't know then how loud a dog's demands could make a man feel, or how stubborn a little ragamuffin could be about what he wanted. But I did know one thing.

For twenty dollars, I'd bought a story—and I had just bought the greatest service dog any funeral home could ever ask for.

Chapter 2 — Mulligan's First Bath

Bringing Mulligan home wasn't exactly like buying the cutest beagle in the pet store. Mulligan—if we're being honest—was a ragamuffin. Not the prettiest dog I'd ever seen. The deal breaker, of course, was that he was a brilliant talking dog, which went a long way toward evening the scales. Still, he needed to look at least somewhat presentable.

I'd had practice in this department.

Years earlier, I bought Julia what I thought was a beautiful collie. You know—Lassie, come to life.

Instead, I showed up at a trailer house about an hour from the funeral home, and what came trotting out was… let's say the ugliest collie I'd ever seen. I should have turned around, but I couldn't leave him there. The place was awful.

So, into the car he went.

About ten minutes down the road, he got carsick. By the time I pulled into the funeral-home parking lot, he'd managed to throw up, relieve himself in every possible way, and coat himself with enough fleas to qualify as a moving insect exhibit.

I figured I'd clean him up before introducing him to Julia. I dragged him into the prep room, rolled up my sleeves, and tried to bathe him. That's when I realized this job was above my pay grade. I needed professionals.

I begged a groomer to take him that day—paid extra, no appointment, the whole deal. I was desperate. This collie wasn't just a dog anymore; he was a test of my marriage.

Finally scrubbed and fluffed, I brought him home, terrified about how Julia would receive him. Would she see the Lassie I'd promised, or the nervous, skittish mutt I'd dragged out of that trailer?

It turned out she saw something better. She saw a dog who needed love—and she gave it.

When Mulligan came along, I already knew the drill: ugly, messy, skittish, liar or not... he was family from day one.

With Mulligan, it was different only in degree. He didn't puke in the car or host a flea convention—the smells this time were mostly good, old-fashioned dog. His problem wasn't sickness; it was style. His coat was coarse and unruly, refusing to lie in any sensible direction.

I took him to the same groomer I'd used for Teddy, with the same urgency and the same financial incentives. I paid extra, promised a small fortune, and left Mulligan for a couple of hours with someone who, on paper, called herself a professional.

When I picked him up, he looked like the same—a bona fide ragamuffin. His fur refused to lie flat, his ears stuck out at angles that offended geometry, and whatever they'd done in the back room made him look like he'd just come out of a bunker at Colonial. The groomer handed me the receipt and shrugged, as if it were the dog's fault.

Back in my office at the funeral home, I shared the plan with Mulligan.

"We're going to break it to Julia gently," I said. "You're going to be the talking dog she never asked for."

Mulligan cocked his head—that half-crooked, half-wise look he had. Then, like he'd been rehearsing for a life of small cons, he leaned forward and began.

"Before I start talking to Julia," he said, with more solemnity than I'd ever heard from a dog, "you need to get me Farah."

He didn't mean a chew toy. He meant the one—the old neighbor's supermodel Afghan hound. Long as a flagpole, prim as a prom queen, and apparently trained to float rather than walk. Mulligan described her like royalty arriving on a parade float: silk coat, topknot tied by some Frenchman in a beret, a handler who whispered commands like poetry.

"You want me to kidnap a show dog?" I asked, because saying it out loud made it easier to refuse.

"Not kidnap, Cole. Rescue." His eyes glinted. "Farah is lonely. She needs a life of honest naps and meatloaf. Also, she's got a topknot I can't stop staring at. And I will not speak to Julia—not one peep—until you agree."

I let that sink in.

I'd just paid a groomer to attempt the impossible and come back with a creature who looked like a construction-site souvenir. Yet here he sat—ragged, ridiculous, and suddenly more demanding than any bereaved cousin I'd ever counseled.

"Cole," I told myself out loud, so Mulligan could hear, "you are not stealing anyone's dog. You officiate funerals. You don't run canine liberation movements."

If I got caught, it wasn't just my freedom on the line—it was our business, the funeral home's reputation, the whole lot. I could see the headlines already: Funeral Director Arrested for Dognapping Supermodel Afghan Hound.

Pun intended. Not funny.

Mulligan, however, had perfected the slow pivot from tall tale to tender plea. The details he rattled off—brush from the skin out, velvet snood, salmon pâté for breakfast—made the whole notion sound ridiculous and oddly plausible all at once. I found myself rehearsing defenses I'd never need, thinking of bail bonds and lawyers and how you explain your absence to families expecting you to preside over a funerals.

He folded his paws like a tiny juror and waited.

I stared at him and felt, for a moment, like the defendant in a case I never planned to try. He was asking me to choose between common sense and romance that would end in, at best, a new sofa cover and, at worst, criminal charges.

The car smelled faintly of shampoo and something older, the way the funeral home does after a long week. I wrapped the towel tighter around my knees and tried to shape the words I'd use on the walk into the living room: honest, quick, and with a bit of humor.

"Julia," I'd say, "I saw a sign that said talking dog for twenty dollars."

That felt like the truth—and nothing like a marriage-saving speech.

Mulligan watched me work through it, then added, almost as an afterthought, "Also, I'm not talking to Julia until this is fixed."

I blinked. "You mean you'll be quiet in front of her?"

"Exactly." He yawned, as if it were a generous concession.

So there it was: the deal. I bought a talking dog for twenty dollars and walked out of a stranger's house with a dog who would not utter a single word in front of my wife until I agreed to help him with something that, by any reasonable measure, sounded like felonious romance.

He sat there—ragged and resolute, tongue lolling—looking very much like a dog who'd already won more arguments than I had that week. I had the unmistakable sensation of being outmaneuvered by a mutt.

"Mulligan," I said finally, "you don't know how lucky you are. Most of Julia's friends joke that if there's reincarnation, they want to come back as one of her pets. You're going to love living with us. We'll take great care of you. Someday, we'll get you a show dog if that's what you want. But we are not stealing Farah—no midnight raids. No puppy-snatching. You get love, food, warmth—and a family."

Just before we left the funeral home to go meet Julia, Mulligan added, very quietly, "I'm not talking until you get me Farah."

And he meant it.

Chapter 3 — Mulligan Makes His Stand

"Mulligan," I said as we turned onto our street, "you've got to talk to Julia. I promise I'll buy you a dog if you really want one. Just help me out, buddy."

He peered up at me with that half-wise, half-mischief look and replied, as if he'd been rehearsing courtroom testimony the whole drive home, "Where's my seat belt?"

"What?"

"My seat belt," he repeated. "I want a real dog seat belt and a booster chair. If you hit the brakes, I bust my nose at best. Go through the window at worst."

I blinked. "There's a seat belt right beside you."

"No," he said patiently. "That's a cinch-it-on. I want a booster and a harness with padding. And while we're at it, premium food. None of that paste stuff. Prime cuts mixed with kibble. I prefer my kibble to be 62.5 percent prime cuts and 37.5 percent filler. Precision matters. Not sixty-two. Not sixty-three. Precision matters."

He said all of this like a man reading from a Michelin guide. I wanted to laugh, but there was Mulligan—earnest as a banker—negotiating creature comforts while I was negotiating morality.

"Fine," I said. "Booster, seat belt, real food—but you give Julia a chance. You say hello to her like a dog with manners."

He sighed. "I'm not talking to Julia until you get me Farah."

"Not happening," I said.

He folded his paws and went quiet, the kind of quiet that tells you Plan B is already fully developed and weaponized. I tried again. No stealing. I promised home-cooked chicken scraps, walks, a yard, and a sunny place to nap. I told him about Teddy and Anna Belle, how they loved the yard, how Julia sometimes cooked for them when she felt indulgent, and how her friends joked they wanted to come back as one of her pets in the next life.

I told Mulligan he'd be loved.

He listened. Then, practical as a man checking his clubs, he said, "Hollywood Feed Store in Dallas has the best stuff. Premium food."

"Got it," I said, because I'd already decided I was susceptible to anyone who used the word premium with authority.

By the time I reached the front walk, I'd rehearsed my speech a dozen ways—ministerial, folksy, apologetic. I smoothed my shirt and went inside.

Julia looked up from her book like surprise arrivals were a misdemeanor she'd already tolerated once. She set the paperback down and peered over her glasses.

"Cole," she said, "what in the world is that?"

"Hey, Julia," I said, aiming for casual. "You're not going to believe this, but I was driving home from a graveside today and saw a sign—Talking dog, twenty dollars. I stopped. I looked. He talked. This is him. His name's Mulligan. Mulligan—do your thing."

Mulligan sat very still.

He did not do his thing.

He did not chirp out his résumé. He did not mention the CIA. He did not acknowledge the room in any meaningful way.

Julia's face narrowed into a look, I know well—the one that has undone more of my good ideas than any leash ever could. "Cole," she said, "we already have two dogs. We don't need a third. And this dog—he's... ugly."

Mulligan growled low, offended in a deeply personal way.

At that moment, Teddy barreled in—our collie, who once came from a trailer house and now looks like a postcard—followed by Anna Belle, who is part beagle, part mischief, and all momentum.

The house erupted.

Teddy barked like a foghorn. Anna Belle contributed a high-pitched trumpet. Mulligan startled and blurted, loud as a sailor, "Holy shit."

Julia's jaw set. "What was that?"

Mulligan attempted a frantic cover-up bark that sounded suspiciously like holy shit with poor diction.

"You heard him," I said before I could stop myself. "He—he spoke."

"Cole," Julia said flatly, "don't be ridiculous."

By now, the dogs were a living cartoon—barking, circling, testing gravity. Teddy launched off the couch with joyful disregard for glass or furniture. One of Julia's glass art pieces—the one she'd paid far too much for and showed visitors like a national treasure—tumbled, then shattered.

Anna Belle, true to form, saw Mulligan as a new opportunity and attempted to hump him with enthusiasm.

It was chaos.

Julia stood in the middle of it—fur, broken glass, overturned cushions—eyes wide.

Then Mulligan did something unexpected.

He let out a bark unlike any I'd ever heard—deep, musical, purposeful. It rolled through the room like a tuning fork struck cleanly.

Teddy froze mid-motion. Anna Belle stopped. Both dogs sat and looked at Mulligan with sudden attention, as if reminded of an appointment they couldn't miss.

"Julia," I said, breathing fast, "I swear he can talk."

She took in the room. The glass. The silence. The two dogs sitting like choirboys. Then she looked at Mulligan, who sat there like a man who'd just played a winning card.

"I don't want him," she said. "Take him back."

I begged like a child. "Please. He'll go with me to the funeral home every day. I'll bathe him, feed him, walk him. You won't have to do a thing."

"So, when you go play golf," she said, "I'll have to feed him."

"Nope. He can come with me."

"You can't bring a dog to Ridglea."

"Yes, I can," I blurted. "I'll get him a service-dog collar. No one refuses a service dog."

Julia stared at me like I'd suggested we retire to Alaska.

She didn't say yes. She didn't say no.

She said she would think about it.

And because of that, I was sure she'd decide the right way. Julia never kept pets out of obligation—only love. I'd seen it too many times to doubt it.

I looked at Mulligan. Ragged. Ridiculous. Entirely unconcerned with human negotiations.

"I'll figure out a legal plan for Farah," I whispered. "But you have to talk to Julia. Just say hello."

He leaned close and whispered back, solemn and sly, "I'm not talking until you get me Farah."

He meant it.

And that's where I found myself: shattered glass at my feet, two dogs sworn to silence, a wife weighing my sanity, and a talking ragamuffin demanding a runway model.

I had a feeling Julia would decide soon.

My bigger problem was figuring out how to get Mulligan to speak in front of the one person whose opinion mattered most.

Chapter 4 — Shopping List for a Canine Diva

The next morning, we rode to the funeral home in a silence that felt like a pause before a lawnmower starts. Mulligan glanced at me, then out the window, then back again—like a man timing his escape from a bad party.

Finally, he spoke.

"Where are we going?"

"To the funeral home," I said.

"No, we're not," he corrected. "We're going to Hollywood Feed. You promised me a dog seat belt, a booster seat, new beds, and anything I wanted."

I sighed. "That was not the promise."

"That was absolutely the promise," he said. "You may not remember it clearly, but I do."

The List

"Not just a seat belt," he continued. "A real one. Booster chair with a padded harness. You hit the brakes; I bust my nose—or go through the windshield. Not negotiable."

"All right," I said, already bracing myself. "Booster and seat belt. Anything else?"

He launched into the list like a man reading from a Neiman Marcus catalog.

"A bed for the funeral home. Another for the house. Retractable leash. Engraved collar. Stainless bowls—Teddy and Anna Belle are sick of their cheap ones and want new Posturepedic beds too—and toys. Lots of toys. Oh, and premium food. You remember my ratio."

"Sixty-two-point-five percent prime cuts," I said.

"Correct. Precision matters."

He said it with the conviction of a sommelier judging kibble.

We were two blocks from the funeral home when he added the kicker.

"And a coat. I'll need a coat here and there."

"This is Texas," I said. "You already have a coat. It's called fur."

"Fur," he sniffed, "is magnificent. It deserves respect—and an overcoat for formal occasions."

I tried not to laugh. Part of me mourned the receipts. The rest of me wanted to see just how far this was going to go.

Dog French 101

"And when we get Farah," Mulligan continued casually, "we'll need Jacqueline. She's Farah's trainer. She's French. Farah only speaks French."

I blinked. "Farah speaks French?"

"Not human French," he said patiently. "Dog French."

"Dog French?" I repeated. "That's a thing?"

"Of course it is. Teddy and Anna Belle only speak Dog English. I tried teaching them some Dog French once—they looked at me like I'd suggested we eat with forks. Jacqueline must be hired. She'll teach them."

I stared at the road. "You want me to rescue a show dog and then hire her French trainer to run a canine language school in our backyard?"

"Exactly," he said, pleased that I understood. "We're not stealing. We're making a cultural exchange. They'll be bilingual in six months."

I pictured Anna Belle attempting to roll her R's and Teddy wearing a beret. The mental soundtrack involved a wheezing accordion.

"You're kidding me, right?"

He smiled—the smile of a dog who had already ordered uniforms.

Calling Fa

I sighed and reached for my phone. "Fine. Let me call Fa—my twin. Her real name is Faye, but when I was three, I couldn't say it right. She's been Fa ever since."

Fa runs the front desk at the funeral home and keeps things moving when I can't. I needed to warn her we would be late—and possibly bankrupt.

Mulligan watched me dial like a general awaiting air support.

"And Cole?"

"Yes?"

"Hollywood Feed has the good harnesses. Go with padding. And choose a premium food that prioritizes protein at the top. I like tuna too, but we don't need to discuss my palate yet."

I laughed despite myself. "You're the strangest customer I've ever had."

"I'm not a customer," he said serenely. "I'm a future good decision."

I called Fa, kept my tone professional, and explained that a "minor delay" was underway. When I hung up, Mulligan was still taking mental inventory.

The Agreement

"All right," I said. "Hollywood Feed. Booster seat, harness, new beds, premium food, fancy collar—and apparently Dog French lessons, if that's the hill you want to die on."

Mulligan thumped his tail, satisfied—the look of a man who had just negotiated a promotion.

Outside, the day was bright, the neighborhood still, and the world contained at least one dog who believed he deserved prime cuts and a beret.

We turned toward Hollywood Feed—me driving, Mulligan dreaming—and neither of us realized that by the time we left, his shopping list would feel less like preparation and more like a declaration of war.

Appraisals, Purchases, and a Runway Dog

Five thousand dollars and two cremations later.. love waft ithe air.

Five thousand dollars and two cremations

Chapter 5 — Appraisals, Purchases, and a Runway Dog

We pulled into the funeral-home lot with a lighter wallet and a heavier conscience.

Hollywood Feed had relieved me of $1,732.54, leaving Mulligan richer in accessories than most college freshmen. He rode in his new booster seat like a man with both a credit line and a calling—bed, harness, monogrammed collar, stainless bowls, toys, and food precise enough to require a spreadsheet.

Pitching the Team

I'd rehearsed my pitch on the drive back.

"Ladies and gentlemen," I'd say, "I have an inspired idea: a service dog for the funeral home. Not just any dog—a talking one. Imagine the comfort. The goodwill. The press."

It sounded ridiculous and brilliant in equal measure.

Fa met us at the door—equal parts twin and truth serum—with the rest of the staff peeking over her shoulder like a small, skeptical jury.

"I was driving back from a graveside," I began, "saw a sign—Talking Dog, twenty dollars. I stopped, I bought him, and he talks. We're… negotiating terms."

They blinked.

Then came the chorus.

"Twenty dollars? For that dog?"

Someone whispered, "That's the ugliest dog I've ever seen."

Mulligan growled low—the kind of growl usually reserved for mailmen and moral failure.

"Perfect," someone muttered. "A service dog that terrifies our families."

I decided leadership required retreat and dignity—mostly retreat.

Mulligan and I ducked into my office.

The Research

He went outside to do his business. I did mine—Googling.

If I were going to acquire a show dog, I needed facts.

Top Afghan hounds ran five to seven thousand dollars, sometimes more. Mulligan's former neighbors—Gladys and Thesby Richardson—were Broadway Baptist royalty. He'd been a bank president. She'd been showing Afghans since Eisenhower.

My search produced ribbons, show notes, and an old newspaper photo: Gladys in pearls, her Afghan shimmering beside her like a comet. One of her dogs had even placed at Westminster.

No wonder Mulligan was smitten.

The research also sent me down a French rabbit hole. Turns out Gladys wasn't "French" in the way Texans sometimes claim Irish ancestry every March—she was the real thing. Three-time president of the French Club, fluent enough to order escargot without pointing, and personally responsible for bringing in Jacqueline Cousteau, Fort Worth's only French dog trainer with Olympic-level eyebrow judgment.

And suddenly my brain reached for the only French connection I had: my grandfather. Half his stories involved France, French family, or French food—and all of them sounded more convincing than they probably were. But in moments like these, a man uses whatever ancestry he's got. Even if it's flimsy ancestry.

Farah herself had been shown a few times but hadn't yet won. That told me two things: she wasn't their top champion, and they knew exactly what she was worth.

So, I formed a plan: start low, offer cash, and sweeten it with something practical. Not bribery—creative problem-solving.

If necessary, throwing in a couple of prepaid cremations with memorial services at Broadway Baptist wouldn't hurt.

Back to Hollywood Feed

Mulligan listened like a campaign donor hearing a strategy. His tail kept time.

"I want to come," he said.

Halfway down Camp Bowie, he went still—the kind of stillness that means the next sentence will cost money.

"Turn around. We forgot Farah's things."

"We just left."

"She'll need a cushion and seat belt. Not a booster—a couture cushion and bling. Her bowl must sparkle. Her leash must glisten. It's a moral issue."

I sighed and turned around.

Another $1,176.85 disappeared—crystals, velvet, and a leash reflective enough to signal aircraft.

The Purchase

At last, we rang the Richardsons' bell.

Mrs. Gladys Richardson answered in pearls and grace. Mulligan trembled beside me like a groom before his first dance.

I launched into my speech—heritage, compassion, the comfort a calm, well-trained dog could bring to grieving families—and then, for reasons still unknown to science, added:

"My grandfather was from France."

Gladys smiled kindly and said they were not selling Farah.

Mulligan's tail fell like the stock market.

Then Mr. Richardson appeared in the hallway.

"How much will you give?"

"Five thousand," I blurted. "Cash. And two fully funded cremations with memorial services at Broadway Baptist."

They exchanged a look. You could almost hear the ledger balancing sentiment against opportunity.

Mr. Richardson nodded and extended his hand.

Just like that, Farah Richardson became Farah Sheridan.

She glided to the car like a duchess boarding Air Force One.

The Ride Home

Farah was everything advertised—silk coat, flawless topknot, a gait like music on marble.

She stepped into the back seat and settled beside Mulligan, who looked up at me as if to say, You're welcome.

I'd moved his booster to the back seat next to her couture cushion. Now he sat belted in, gazing at her like a man who'd married well above his station.

As the funeral home came into view, I glanced at them—one scruffy and grinning, one regal and radiant—and realized I'd spent more on dogs in forty-eight hours than I really wanted to calculate.

And somehow, it still didn't feel like a mistake.

Of course, I didn't yet know that by morning, Farah would have the entire funeral-home staff eating out of her paw—

and Mulligan would be taking the credit.

Chapter 6 — Back-Seat Nuptials

We were only a few minutes from the funeral home when I started to hear a soft, strange little cooing coming from the back seat.

At first, I thought Anna Belle had hidden a squeaky toy back there. Then I realized it was Mulligan, rubbing his head against Farah's flank like a teenage couple at a drive-in movie.

If I closed my eyes for half a second, I could have sworn I heard the faintest burble of something that might be called Dog French. That realization scared the holy living daylights out of me—mostly because I noticed I was actively listening for Dog French.

Then Mulligan blurted, loud as a man announcing last call at a bar,

"Patron!"

"What?" I said.

"We should call you Patron."

"No, buddy. Patron is tequila."

"No, dummy," he said patiently. "Patrón is the boss in French. My first boss was Jefe—that's Spanish for boss. Farah is French. She wants to call you Patron."

He pronounced it like it was both flattering and inevitable.

"Farah isn't French," I said, clinging to the last threads of reason. "She's an Afghan hound. Afghanistan."

"No, she isn't," Mulligan replied with the confidence of someone who'd verified this information by scent. "She's French."

"Fine," I said. "If you want her to be French, she's French."

I was too tired to argue with a dog's geography.

Evian and Engagements

Mulligan wasn't finished. He leaned closer, whispering in the same conspiratorial tone my barber uses right before a bad haircut.

"Patron, Farah wants to know what kind of water you have?"

"What kind of water?"

"The kind that comes out when you turn the handle?"

"That won't do," he said gravely. "Farah only drinks Evian. Not from the big bottles—they go bad. Little bottles. Fresh. Frequently."

"You're kidding," I said. "Water doesn't go bad."

"Have you ever drunk day-old toilet water?" he shot back. "Exactly. Tastes like shit."

I pulled into the nearest convenience store, took out my wallet, and bought a case of small Evian bottles.

By the time I got back to the car, a full council was in session—sniffing, soft howling, and what sounded suspiciously like applause.

I opened the door. Mulligan and Farah were practically vibrating.

"She said yes," Mulligan announced.

I stared at them, buckled into booster seats, vibrating with joy, and wondered how my life had veered this far off the map in under forty-eight hours.

"She said yes to what?"

"I asked her to marry me."

I blinked. "Congratulations. You're… married?"

"Not yet," Mulligan said, patient as a professor explaining quantum physics to a Labrador. "We must have a wedding. Not in some park—a proper chapel. Your chapel is perfect. And a reception. Your reception hall will do. Elegant. Tasteful. With napkins."

"You want a wedding in my chapel?" I asked, picturing flower arrangements and visitation chairs. "Who's coming to this?"

Mulligan didn't hesitate.

"Some of my old buddies—Jefe's crew. Diesel, Rex, Bruiser, Scar, Rocco, Knox, Blaze, Ghost, Grit, Havoc, Vex, Bandit, Ruger, Snoop, Glock, Chaos, Diablo, Biggie, Capone, Rico, Tito, Vito, and Cash."

"And her friends?" I asked weakly.

"The supermodels," Mulligan said dreamily. "Bella, Coco, Giselle, Sofia, Amélie, Chantal, Juliette, Vivienne, Colette, Dior, Chanel, Fifi, Bijou, Fleur, Lune, Élodie, Babette, Noëlle, Lola, Paris, Chérie, Mimi, Brigitte, Louboutin, and Margaux."

He recited the list like a dog reading Vogue. I laughed despite myself.

"Okay," I said finally. "But we are absolutely not having a gang-and-glamour wedding in my chapel this weekend."

"We don't have that long," Mulligan said solemnly. "Gestations last about sixty days."

"Gestation?" I said.

I stared at them, buckled into booster seats, vibrating with joy, and wondered how my life had veered this far off the map in under forty-eight hours.

The Ultimatum

"Nope. Nope. Nope," I said, making the same face Julia uses when I suggest mauve paint. "I don't want to hear about gestation periods. That's weird, it's gross, and I'm not announcing your progeny from the pulpit."

Mulligan leaned back, crossed his paws, and began a chant that would have embarrassed a preschooler.

"La la la la, I can't hear you."

Farah gave me a patient look and then added, delicately,

"Nous voulons un beau mariage, dans votre chapelle, Patron, avec une réception très élégante dans votre salle de réception."

Mulligan translated proudly.

"She says, 'We want a beautiful wedding in your chapel, Patron, with an exquisite reception in your reception hall.'"

My head spun. The car smelled of shampoo, leather, and now the faint perfume of wedding planning. I pictured my chapel filled with tuxedoed dogs, my reception hall serving kibble hors d'oeuvres on silver trays, and Fa trying to manage the seating chart.

"Listen," I said. "We'll do this slowly. No weddings this week. No guest list the size of a minor kingdom. And for heaven's sake, no counting backward."

Mulligan tilted his head like a bishop considering doctrine.

"We'll work out the details over the next few days," he said.

"But hurry, Patron. Time matters."

The name stuck to me like dog hair on a black suit. I wasn't sure whether to be insulted or honored.

"Okay," I said at last. "We'll start with Evian and maybe—just maybe—we'll talk about the rest after I consult with Julia."

Mulligan closed his eyes and sighed like a man who trusted in Fate, Kibble, and the persuasive power of a perfect topknot.

"La la la la," he sang softly. "I can't hear you."

I wasn't sure whether he was refusing to listen—or whether I was refusing to say no. Either way, we'd better clean the chapel.

What I didn't yet realize was that by the next morning, Fa would have the chapel booked, Julia would have opinions, and Mulligan would already be working on a seating chart.

Chapter 7 — Two at a Time

We pulled into the funeral-home lot, and I turned to Mulligan.

"All right," I said. "I've done my part. Now you do yours. When I introduce you and Farah to the staff, you are not going to make me look like I've lost my mind. You talk. You explain that Farah doesn't speak human, but if anyone needs to tell her something, you can translate. And we figure out how you two can be the best service dogs this funeral home has ever seen. Agreed?"

Mulligan wagged his tail like a man closing a deal.

"Okay," he said. "As long as we start planning the wedding—and it's within a week. We don't want people counting backward if, well… time matters."

I blinked. "Wedding? We're talking about staff introductions first, Mulligan. Baby steps."

The Introduction

We walked into the reception room. The staff looked at me the way they always do when I act on impulse—equal parts amusement and mild alarm.

Fa was at the coffee urn, doing what Fa does best: holding the world together with cookies and a smile.

"Everyone," I said, clapping once for attention, "little announcement. As I mentioned yesterday, I was driving back from the Smiths' graveside and saw a sign that said Talking Dog—$20. I stopped. I bought him. Yes, he can talk. Also—he's crafty. Yesterday, he tried to blackmail me into stealing an Afghan from his old neighbors. I didn't steal her. I bought her fair and square."

I gestured toward Mulligan and Farah, who stood side by side like an oddly matched royal couple.

"So, we're getting not one, but two service dogs. Mulligan talks. Farah speaks Dog French."

The room went still—the kind of silence usually reserved for visitations at dawn. I felt my face warm.

"Yes, I know," I said quickly. "Dog French sounds insane. But there's Dog English, Dog French—possibly Dog Swahili. Just hang on."

"Mulligan," I said, because at that point there was no retreat, "come on up."

Mulligan Tells His Story

He cleared his throat and began like a seasoned storyteller.

"When I was a pup," he said, "I worked for a man named Jefe—long story, bad hours, paid in bones."

The room leaned in.

"Then, one afternoon, Farah trotted past like she'd bought the world and sold the receipts—silk coat, aristocratic carriage, a topknot that made hats look lazy. I fell in love. We married, had puppies, and with my rugged charm and her runway face, our pups looked like magazine covers. People paid fifteen grand apiece."

A few eyebrows lifted.

"A photographer took a family shot. Next thing I knew, I was on the cover of Canine Vogue. Producers called. Could I look soulful and suspicious in one take? Before long, I was a stunt dog—jumps, slow-motion runs, fake glass, the works."

Farah stood serenely, as if she'd heard this before.

"She liked the ribbons until a rubber chandelier incident convinced her to ask for a quieter life. So I trained dogs. I can teach a dog to heel in a day and a handler to think three weeks ahead. I speak Dog and Human—handy at gravesides, even handier in dressing rooms."

He paused, then smiled.

"That's the long and short of it: noisy, glamorous, ridiculous. I can sit still in a storm, make a stranger in a chapel breathe out a laugh, and I like salmon pâté and padded booster seats."

Then he turned to the staffer who had called him ugly.

"And to the guy who said I was ugly—next time, I'll bite your ass, fatso."

For half a heartbeat, silence.

Then Fa—who has no filter when animals are involved—darted forward, scooped Farah under the chin, and started loving on her.

That broke the spell.

The rest of the staff followed, circling the dogs like a tide. Someone tested Mulligan's sit. Someone else admired Farah's coat. She tolerated it all with the calm of practiced fame.

"Hey," Mulligan said, rolling his eyes, "cut it out with the baby talk. In dog years, we're older than some of you."

Laughter erupted.

The introduction worked better than I dared hope. Even the skeptics smiled. Fa whispered something about making a sign for the Sheridan Calm Canine Program. I pretended not to hear her.

The Next Challenge

When things settled, I slipped into the hallway like a man escaping a committee meeting. Mulligan followed and sat at my feet, tail thumping.

"Good job," I said. "You delivered. But now—Julia. Anna Belle and Teddy. You and Farah. How do I get you all home without Julia thinking I've lost my mind again?"

Mulligan gave me that careful, calculating look he reserves for negotiations involving prime cuts.

"We'll charm her," he said. "Start small. Let her meet me alone first. Then Farah. The ceremony can wait."

I sighed, picturing sensible, patient Julia opening the door to find two royal strays in her living room. The logistics alone were terrifying: more bowls, more beds, and another shattered sculpture waiting to happen.

"We'll do it your way," I said. "Slow. No chapel-before-consent weddings. No guest lists. No Evian orders on day one."

Mulligan thumped his tail once, sealing the bargain.

"And Patron," he said, "start practicing your toast."

Patron. The name clung to me.

I looked at him, at Farah, at the hallway that led toward Julia—and beyond it, an ordinary Tuesday that was about to turn spectacularly un-ordinary.

"Okay," I said. "Let's go home."

The Rehearsal

We walked back through the reception hall, past Fa—who was already sketching banner ideas—through the kitchenette, and out to the parking lot.

I had a car full of dogs, a staff full of stories, and a wife who valued order. Somehow, I had to make those worlds meet in the middle.

On the drive home, I rehearsed my pitch with the care I usually reserve for eulogies: polite, honest, and just charming enough. If Mulligan and Farah were going to stay, I'd have to sell the idea to the one person whose opinion mattered most.

I only hoped my voice would hold.

What I did not know was that before I could open my mouth, Mulligan had already scheduled the first family "meeting"—and Julia was about to meet the most persuasive talking dog in Texas.

Chapter 8 — The Re-Introduction

By the time we pulled into the driveway, the sun had dipped low and buttery—one of those Fort Worth evenings that makes even your worst ideas look handsome in the right light. Farah sat like royalty in the back seat, all silk and cheekbones. Mulligan—new harness, engraved collar, and a surplus of confidence—watched the front door like a man about to pitch investors.

"Ground rules," I said. "We walk in calm. No weddings. No Evian negotiations. And you, Mulligan—you talk. You promised."

He thumped his tail once. "Patron," he said, solemn as a judge, "I will deliver."

Julia opened the door with a look that suggested she had counted the dogs we owned that morning and did not expect the number to change by dinner. Teddy ambled up behind her, all collie hospitality and earnest concern. Anna Belle arrived like a joyful misdemeanor.

"Cole," Julia said slowly, "why do you have two dogs with you?"

I cleared my throat. "Well… technically, one is new-new. The other is new-ish. Julia, I'd like to reintroduce you to Mulligan. He has something to—" I pivoted, pointed, and hoped the gesture read as supportive rather than desperate. "—do your thing."

Mulligan stepped forward, sat square, and looked my wife directly in the eye.

"Good evening," he said, crisp as a linen napkin. "I'm Mulligan, and I'm a talking dog."

Julia blinked. Teddy froze mid–tail wag. Anna Belle sat. For a full beat, the house held its breath.

Then, very calmly, Julia said, "No."

"Respectfully," Mulligan replied, "yes."

He turned to Teddy and Anna Belle and let out one low, musical bark—the parishioners-please-be-seated bark. Both dogs folded neatly at his flanks. Farah slipped past me and arranged herself on the rug like an afterthought from a perfume ad—one that costs more when you pronounce it without moving your lips.

Julia lowered her glasses and stared. I could feel the moment teetering between Are you out of your mind and All right, I'm listening.

Mulligan's "Short" Version

"May I tell you my story?" Mulligan asked. "The short version."

I knew that was a lie on par with I'll be right back after Costco.

Julia folded her arms. "I'm listening."

"When I was a pup," he began, "I belonged to an evil man named Jefe. He fed me well and used me poorly. I sat in rooms—tail down, ears open—collecting conversations. Who was skimming. Who owed what. Who planned betrayal. I was useful, which is a lonely thing to be when you're young."

The room leaned in.

"One night at his clubhouse—the Drug Dealers' Clubhouse," he clarified, as if it had an HOA, "I overheard a rival planning to execute Jefe as he walked out. I warned him. I didn't know one of the rival's men was in the next stall."

He paused.

"The shouting starts. Doors fly open. Suddenly the place becomes a noise museum—Glocks, AKs, a chandelier that never hurt anyone. Everybody shooting at everybody, nobody hitting the ice machine."

Anna Belle crept closer.

"I ran," Mulligan said quietly. "Bullets biting dirt on both sides. I ran until my legs gave out and the world went still."

"When I woke up, I was under a tree with a plaque that said The Hanging Tree, on a hill overlooking Fort Worth. A golf course. I followed the fairway—dogleg right—hid from rattlesnakes and coyotes and found a man in an ivy cap and tweed trousers hitting balls at a boy who couldn't catch."

He smiled.

"The boy missed another ball. I couldn't stand it. I trotted out, caught one on the first bounce, and set it in the towel like a baby bird. The man stared. 'I wish I could hire you as my shag boy,' he said."

"'I'm recently unemployed,' I told him. 'What's the pay?'"

Teddy let out a reverent whuff.

"'Well, I'll be,' he said. 'A talking dog. I'm Ben Hogan.'"

Even Julia's mouth twitched.

"For a while, he took me in. Named me Shaggy. Best job I ever had. When Mr. Hogan passed, his yardman kept me. Then the yardman's son—who had troubles—took me back to my old boss."

Mulligan nodded once.

"Jefe listened to my escape story, then said, 'Well, I guess I got a Mulligan.' And so I did."

He turned to Farah, who sat so beautifully I wanted to tip her.

"And then she appeared. Farah. I fell in love as fast as a dog spots a steak. I imagined puppies—her elegance, my conversation skills. Twenty-five thousand a pup. More if they could pronounce charcuterie."

Farah flicked an ear. Julia rolled her eyes toward heaven—the one she uses when something is ridiculous and, somehow, happening.

The Case for Staying

"This," I said weakly, gesturing at the room, "is where I explain how they ended up in the back of my car."

"Allow me," Mulligan said. "Patron did not kidnap Farah. He negotiated. There were cash considerations and dignified arrangements suitable for two adults of standing. We came home properly."

"Properly," Julia repeated.

"Also," Mulligan added, "Farah prefers small bottles of Evian."

"Mulligan."

"What? Hydration matters."

Julia looked from me to Farah—her coat, her posture—then back to Mulligan, who sat like he was auditioning for Reasonable Dog.

"I need to understand something," she said. "Why should these dogs live in this house?"

Mulligan dipped his head. The showmanship evaporated.

"Because we can help," he said. "When rooms get loud with grief, I can make them quiet. I can sit beside someone who's about to break and remind them to breathe. I can make Teddy and Anna Belle listen when they forget how. And I can make you laugh when you haven't in a week."

He glanced at Farah.

"She is beauty where the world has been ugly. She gives people something lovely to look at when their eyes are tired from crying. She doesn't speak human, but she understands posture—and sometimes posture is what keeps us upright."

Teddy pressed his shoulder into Julia's leg. Anna Belle edged closer, tail sweeping the baseboard.

The pitch landed. Soft. Honest.

House Rules

"All right," Julia said at last. "Trial basis. And if either of you breaks any more art, you're sleeping in the hearse."

"Understood," Mulligan said. "Tap water, decanted with dignity."

"I'll take them to the funeral home every day," I said. "They'll work."

Julia studied Farah's topknot like it had applied for credit in our name. Then she bent, palm down. Farah touched her fingers with her nose soft as velvet on Sunday shoes.

"Welcome," Julia said.

Mulligan cleared his throat. "One small administrative item."

"No," Julia and I said together.

"Then I'll save it for the staff meeting."

He swallowed the rest like a pill—grudgingly, with cheese.

Settling In

Bowls were set down. Beds dragged into corners. The back door opened. Teddy escorted Farah like a gentleman. Anna Belle hovered, torn between jealousy and awe. Mulligan paused at the threshold and looked back.

"Thank you," he said.

"Don't make me regret it," Julia replied.

Later, he came in first, sat before her, and spoke without giving a performance.

"I've told tall tales," he said. "But this part is simple. I belong here. If you'll have me, I'll earn it."

Julia scratched behind his ear. "Earn it."

The house settled into a quiet I hadn't heard in a while—no bargaining, no lists, no chapel reservations—just the clean hush of a promise made.

From the hall, Farah coughed delicately.

"Administrative item?" Mulligan whispered.

"Fine," Julia sighed. "What?"

"Place cards for dinner."

"Go lie down."

And for once, he did.

He curled at her feet like he had finally reached the place he'd been running toward since a crooked sign on a post changed both our lives.

Somewhere in the quiet, I heard myself rehearsing a toast I was not ready to give.

I didn't know it yet, but by morning the chapel phones would start ringing—and Mulligan's first official assignment would arrive with more cameras than casseroles.

Chapter 9 — Contract Negotiations

In Which a Talking Dog Attempts to Unionize the Funeral Home

The next morning, Mulligan, Farah, and I headed to the funeral home. The two of them were in the back seat again—pawing, preening, whispering what I was now convinced was Dog French, which is like regular French but with more rolling r's and the occasional romantic growl.

Farah looked like she'd stepped off a Paris runway. Mulligan looked like he'd slept on $1,700 worth of orthopedic bedding—which, technically, he had.

Halfway down Camp Bowie, Mulligan cleared his throat with the pomp of a man about to accept a lifetime achievement award.

"So, Patron... how about last night?"

He leaned back in his booster seat like he owned the car. "Pretty smooth and debonair, wasn't it?"

I checked the rearview mirror. "You did great, buddy. But I hate to break it to you—Mr. Hogan died over thirty years ago. If Julia decides to Google you, you're busted."

Mulligan sat up straighter, offended. "Google ruins everything."

"How did you even know all that Ben Hogan stuff anyway?"

He flashed the guilty-proud grin of someone who has committed a crime but believes society benefited.

"I read it in his book."

I blinked. "You can read?"

"Read? Heck yes. English, Spanish, Italian, French—and I'm learning Pig Latin."

"Where did you even find Hogan's book?"

Mulligan gazed out the window like a telenovela star preparing to reveal a dark family secret.

"There's something I haven't told you about Jefe."

Of course, there was.

"By night," he said, lowering his voice, "Jefe was a drug lord. But by day? A surgeon from Mexico. Top tier. He's been blackmailed by the cartels for years. Two obsessions: medicine... and Ben Hogan."

I nearly rear-ended a Kia.

"His home office looked like a Hogan museum," Mulligan continued. "Signed photographs everywhere—the one-iron at Merion, the cover of Power Golf, swing sequences from Modern Fundamentals. I read them all. If I had hands, I'd be on tour."

He paused, because Mulligan loved pausing for effect.

"And Jefe was so eaten up with Hogan he dressed like him. Gray slacks. White shirts. Cashmere sweaters. The cap. He'd shower, put on his Hogan clothes, and leave through a private tunnel he built under his house—one mile long—to sneak off to his Dallas country club."

"A tunnel?" I sputtered.

"Of course. Most dealers sleep all day. Jefe joined a Jewish country club under the name Jonathan Goldsmith. They liked him so much he converted, became a lay rabbi, and volunteers at Jewish Family Services."

I covered my mouth. "Mulligan... this is the most ridiculous story I've ever heard."

He shrugged. "They'd buy him a Dos Equis and call him the most interesting man they'd ever met."

I laughed. "Stop."

"Can't," he said. "Truth doesn't take breaks."

He thumped his tail once, satisfied with himself. Then he added, casually, "Anyway, before we get to the funeral home, we need to stop by Hollywood Feed again."

My head snapped around. "Why? We were there twice yesterday."

"For Farah," he said solemnly. "She needs a new collar and a few other things."

"She just got a new collar yesterday."

"Exactly. That one's from you. This one's from me. It's a wedding gift."

"Mulligan," I said, "you do realize it's me—your Patron—who's paying for all this?"

He brightened. "That reminds me! Since Farah and I are now full-time service dogs, we should discuss compensation."

"Compensation," I repeated.

"Not minimum wage," he continued. "We want good health insurance, vacation time, a 401(k), and a few other things."

"Vacation time?" I said. "You sleep eighteen hours a day."

He ignored that completely. "I have a number in mind. You think of yours. We compare. If we're close, great. If not—kapesh. No talking."

I tried not to laugh. "Anything else you need at Hollywood Feed?"

"Farah needs toys. And I saw this incredible Dog Ball Ejector."

"We don't need a ball ejector. We can throw the ball."

He smirked. "It's not for me. It's for the staff. I drop the ball; they chase it and bring it back. Fatso especially needs the exercise."

I rubbed my temples. "Mulligan... Larry is not chasing a ball."

"We'll see," he said, pleased.

At this point, I was merely a chauffeur in my own life—driving around Fort Worth with a talking dog, a French supermodel Afghan, and a wedding brewing that might require place cards and a harpist.

Terms & Conditions

We were three lights from the funeral home when Mulligan reached under his booster cushion and produced a folded sheet of paper like a lawyer sliding evidence across the table.

"Draft agreement," he announced. "Highlights include premium kibble at the established 62.5 percent protein-to-carb ratio, one small Evian per special occasion, office access during business hours, and 'reasonable accommodations' for Dog French literacy."

"Reasonable accommodations?" I echoed.

He nodded. "Signage. Dual-language place cards for team meetings. Dog English / Dog French."

I pinched the bridge of my nose. "And your number?"

Mulligan smiled like a lobbyist on retainer. "We reveal simultaneously. Transparency builds trust."

The Counteroffer

I parked, turned around, and gave him my best Funeral Director Voice of Authority.

"Here's my offer: room, board, medical care, and more love than any dog has ever needed. In return, you stay groomed, calm, and kind. You keep the family company. You don't break Julia's art. And you do not unionize the staff."

Mulligan turned to Farah and whispered in urgent Dog French. She nodded once—gracefully, like a swan approving a merger.

He looked back at me.

"Add two items," he said. "Hazard pay for children under five… and salmon pâté Fridays."

"Pâté is not a weekday."

"It is now."

"We'll discuss," I said, exhausted.

The Email That Changed Everything

I unlocked my office, sat down, and opened my inbox—ready for invoices, flower orders, and one more reminder about the crematory permit renewal.

Instead, at the top, in bold, was an email from a grieving family:

We heard your funeral home has a talking service dog. Would he be willing to help our son at tomorrow's visitation?

I stared at the screen.

Beside me, Mulligan hopped onto the chair like a junior partner ready to bill hours.

"Well, Patron," he said, straightening his imaginary tie, "looks like my first official contract just came in."

Farah flicked her tail, as if to say:

Showtime.

Chapter 10 — Of Rabbis, Priests & Dog Ball Ejectors

The next morning, the funeral home looked less like a Monday and more like a royal homecoming.

Every staff member was gathered at the front doors like they were expecting dignitaries—or at least a celebrity retriever.

Mulligan stepped out first, chest puffed, fur gleaming like a show dog who'd discovered both religion and conditioner. Farah followed, elegant as ever, her coat catching the sunlight like liquid silk. If there'd been a red carpet, she would have paused halfway down it for photos.

Fa and the team swarmed instantly.

"Who's a handsome boy?"

"Who's my beautiful girl?"

Mulligan groaned. "Patron," he muttered, "they're talking to us like we're toddlers with trust funds."

"Technically," I said, "you kind of are."

I went back to the car to unload our latest haul from Hollywood Feed—our third trip in two days. The trunk looked like Santa's sleigh for spoiled dogs.

Among the treasures were premium collars, organic snacks, monogrammed chew toys, and the pièce de résistance: a gleaming Dog Ball Ejector Deluxe 3000, which promised hands-free interactive play for the discerning pet.

The Demonstration

"Patron," Mulligan said solemnly, "set it up right here in the lobby. It's for staff morale."

"Staff morale?" I said. "This is a funeral home, Mulligan—not recess."

He ignored me, directing like a movie producer.

"A little to the left. Good. Plug it in. Now—observe greatness."

He placed a ball on the launcher, pressed the paw pad, and—THWACK!—a neon tennis ball rocketed across the carpet, grazed the fern by the guest book, and smacked into the far wall.

To my astonishment, every employee—professionals in suits—took off after it.

Larry. Fa. Even our embalmer, Randy, dove like retrievers competing for a promotion.

Mulligan watched, satisfied.

"And they say dogs are the easy ones to train."

By the tenth round, Larry was bent over, wheezing.

"Enough!" I barked. "We've got visitations in an hour, not the Puppy Bowl!"

The staff scattered back to their posts. Mulligan adjusted his tie.

"See, Patron? A little joy never killed a funeral home."

"Close call," I said, watching Larry drain a bottle of water like a man rescued from the desert.

The Officiants

We retreated to my office. I barely sat down before Mulligan clapped his paws together like a CEO.

"Wedding logistics, Patron. We need officiants."

I groaned. "You cannot be serious."

"As a dog bite," he said, "I'm Jewish—I'll need a rabbi. Farah's Catholic—she'll want a priest. Tradition matters."

I rubbed my temples. "So, you're planning a multi-faith canine wedding… in a funeral chapel."

"Exactly," he said brightly. "It'll be historic. I still have Jonathan's number—the rabbi."

"And my brother's a priest," I muttered.

"Perfect! The first priest and rabbi to marry two dogs. The jokes write themselves."

He leaned back, already rehearsing.

"A priest and a rabbi walk into a chapel to officiate a wedding. The priest says, 'I've done some strange services, but this one's ruff.' The rabbi nods, 'At least they've been through obedience school—that's premarital counseling.'"

I buried my face in my hands. "Lord help me."

Enter Jacqueline

"Farah's maid of honor will be Jacqueline," Mulligan continued.

"The French trainer?"

"The only human fluent in Dog French. She understands Farah's emotional range—and my managerial needs."

"You're… what?"

"Managerial. You'll call her. I'll translate. Use this script."

He handed me a notecard covered in perfect cursive French. I stared at it like an alien equation.

"You're kidding."

"I'm not. Practice: Bonjour, je m'appelle Cole Sheridan…"

It took twenty minutes, six attempts, and one near stroke before I got through the phrase without inventing a new language.

Mulligan beamed. "Excellent. You sound like an extra from Les Misérables. Call her now."

So I did. Jacqueline answered in a flurry of elegant French. I caught three words—two of them Farah and magnifique. When she finished, her tone sounded delighted.

Mulligan wagged. "She can't wait to see Farah again. We're in."

The Assignment

I slumped back in my chair. "Talking dog, twenty dollars, my behind."

Before I could reclaim my dignity, my inbox chimed.

A family had written to ask whether our talking service dog might help calm their anxious son during tomorrow's visitation.

Mulligan's expression softened.

"Patron," he said quietly, "my first official case."

I looked at him, at Farah, and at the Dog Ball Ejector sitting in the corner like a trophy from madness.

"Yep," I said. "And for the record—you're officially on salary. Kind of."

He grinned. "I knew we'd reach an agreement."

Outside, the lobby still smelled faintly of tennis balls and chaos. Inside, the world's most unlikely therapy team had just landed its first client.

Chapter 11 — Bonjour, Agent Canin Spécial

Before meeting Jacqueline, I decided to do a little research. A quick Google search turned into a deep dive worthy of the CIA.

Her name was Jacqueline Cousteau. I assumed there had to be a connection to that Cousteau—the ocean guy.

Nope.

Her husband was Ian Anderson Cousteau: filmmaker, rock musician, diver, and—apparently—the man behind Jethro Tull. Not Aqualung the scuba reference, but Aqualung the song about the unsettling fellow on the park bench.

Yes. That one.

So, our French dog trainer was married to a rock legend–oceanographer–philosopher hybrid who lived in Westover Hills. Of course she was. That's how my life works now: a talking dog, a French supermodel Afghan, and a Cousteau household waiting at the end of the driveway.

Their home looked exactly as you'd expect—French Provincial perfection. White stone walls, blue shutters, a courtyard that smelled faintly of lavender…and money.

"Try not to embarrass me," I muttered to Mulligan as we walked up the path.

"Relax," he said. "You're with professionals now."

I wasn't sure if he meant himself or Farah.

I rang the doorbell. It played, Clair de Lune. Naturally.

Jacqueline opened the door, saw Farah, and screamed "Farah!" before launching into a torrent of French that sounded like a champagne-fueled auction. Farah barked back joyfully, tail wagging. It was a reunion of operatic proportions.

Then Jacqueline turned to me and said something that, judging by the hand gestures, meant come inside before you faint.

I cleared my throat and bravely delivered the French sentence Mulligan had drilled into me for an hour:

« Salut ! Je m'appelle Cole Sheridan… c'est mon pote Mulligan ici qui a tout traduit pour moi. Oui, oui—le chien. »

Translation: Hi, I'm Cole. The dog helped me write this. Please don't ask follow-up questions.

Jacqueline blinked twice. Then she looked down at Mulligan.

He stepped forward, bowed slightly, and said,

« Bonjour, madame. Je m'appelle Mulligan, et je suis un chien qui parle. »

Jacqueline fainted.

I caught her before she hit the floor and eased her onto a velvet sofa that probably cost more than my last set of custom golf clubs. Farah hopped up beside her, resting her head gently on Jacqueline's chest like a therapy dog who had clocked in for duty.

When Jacqueline came to, she blinked up at us. Mulligan sat at her feet, polished and composed.

"I'm terribly sorry to startle you," he said. "But yes—I really am a talking dog. You probably have questions."

Le Pitch

Mulligan began speaking in flawless French. I followed along on my phone, watching Google Translate work itself into a mild panic.

"Allow me to explain how I came to speak perfect French," he said.

"It began one humid Dallas morning. Jefe and I were playing golf—long story, bad hours, paid in bones. The course was lovely. The coffee was terrible. We were paired with the French ambassador—a charming man whose backswing resembled someone swatting a mosquito with a baguette."

"On the seventh hole, he overheard me complaining about Texas humidity—in flawless French. He dropped his nine-iron and cried, Mon Dieu ! Un chien qui parle français !"

"By the following week, I was in Paris with a badge that read Agent Canin Spécial. My first mission involved the Paris Olympics—bomb-sniffing, coded poodle interception, the usual."

Even Farah looked impressed.

"Then," Mulligan continued, "Tom Cruise was scheduled to parachute into the opening ceremony for Mission: Impossible. He got cold feet. So they used footage of me instead, put his face on it, and I became the first dog to jump from ten thousand feet wearing a beret."

Jacqueline whispered, "Incroyable."

"Afterward," Mulligan said, "the President of France invited me to dinner at the Élysée Palace. They served duck confit and called me le héros poilu—the hairy hero."

Jacqueline nodded slowly, as if deciding whether to accept this as truth or performance art.

"Eventually, I returned to Texas. One sunny day, Jefe and I were driving down Camp Bowie—top down, wind in my fur—when I saw her."

He turned to Farah.

"The most beautiful creature I'd ever seen. Riding shotgun in your car, Jacqueline. Her ears shimmered like silk. I knew my espionage days were over."

Farah sighed like a film star recalling her breakout role.

"I jumped from the window," Mulligan continued. "Spent three days outside your fence, surviving on rainwater and leftover brisket. On the fourth day, a neighbor left me food—and when I thanked him out loud, he hasn't spoken since."

Terms with Jacqueline

Jacqueline sat up slowly.

"Monsieur Sheridan," she said in English, "I have trained dogs for twenty years. I have seen obedience, disobedience, and even possession—but never... conversation."

"Well," I said, "we're a little different around here."

"And what exactly would this training involve?"

Mulligan grinned. "Oh, the basics. Sit. Stay. Roll over. And teaching Anna Belle and Teddy Dog French."

"Pardon?"

"It'll make sense later," I said quickly.

Jacqueline crossed herself and murmured something that sounded like a request for divine patience.

"Very well," she said. "I will do it."

And just like that, we had a maid of honor, a new trainer, and the first international incident ever sparked by a talking dog.

As we walked back to the car, Mulligan looked smug.

"See, Patron? I told you it would go swimmingly."

"Swimmingly?" I said. "You're just saying that because her husband wrote Aqualung."

Mulligan smirked. "You have to admit—the man has range. Maybe he'll play the wedding."

Back at the funeral home, an email waited.

The family with the anxious boy had confirmed for tomorrow and asked whether our Agent Canin Spécial could meet him today to practice.

Chapter 12 — Dinner Is Served (and So Are the Demands)

That night at home, I could tell Julia was finally warming up to our new "children." Anna Belle and Teddy had embraced their new roles as mentors, teaching Mulligan and Farah the highest art form known to domesticated animals:

How to Get Julia to Do Exactly What You Want

Four dogs curled up in the den looked like a Hallmark movie, the kind that ends with gentle snowfall, a heartfelt lesson, and an overdraft alert.

The Central Market Coup

On the way home, I eased toward Tom Thumb.

Mulligan barked once—sharp, immediate, and morally offended.

"Absolutely not. We're Central Market dogs now."

"Since when?" I asked.

"Since taste and standards became important," he replied, as if explaining gravity.

So, I turned toward the one grocery store where the air smells faintly of imported rosemary and every shopper carries a canvas tote embroidered with a vegetable pun.

An hour later, I stumbled out holding ingredients suitable for a French embassy banquet—plus a receipt that looked like it needed congressional approval.

$462.15

(Not including Farah's truffle garnish or Mulligan's Evian subscription.)

The Feeding Operations Center

When we got home, Julia set the dinner table while I tackled the new nightly ritual: feeding four dogs with four different psychologies, palates, and legal demands.

To preserve what remained of my sanity, I created a laminated master feeding guide.

If you're going to lose control of your home,

you might as well lose it with a gloss finish.

THE SHERIDAN FAMILY CANINE CULINARY PROGRAM

(Now accepting Michelin stars and Milk-Bone endorsements)

Anna Belle — "The Delicate Flower with the Cast-Iron Bark"

Stomach: Sensitive

Motto: If it's bland, it's grand

- Poached chicken with goat yogurt
- Steamed basmati rice (never jasmine)
- Chamomile tea served at 102°F

Deviation results in sighing, pacing, and a side-eye capable of curdling dairy.

Teddy — "The All-Boy, Red-Meat, Rough-and-Tumble Texan"

Stomach: Steel

Motto: If it once mooed, oinked, or clucked, I'll eat it.

- Steak and eggs
- Elk or bison chili (no beans—he's "watching carbs")
- Cowboy ribeye with sweet-potato fries

Eats like John Wayne. Burps like a freight train.

Mulligan — "The Precision Palate of a Golf-Course Spy"

Stomach: Highly opinionated

Motto: Precision matters

- Wagyu medallions (62.5% prime, 37.5% holistic kibble)
- Pan-seared salmon with Maldon salt
- Filet mignon cut into golf-ball-sized spheres
- Sunday dessert: one spoon of French vanilla

(Only with Farah's written approval)

Any ratio slip triggers a formal grievance with HR

(Human Resources Retriever).

Farah — "The Runway Afghan and Culinary Muse of Versailles"

Stomach: Immaculate

Motto: If it sparkles, I'll sample it

- Quail-egg omelet whipped counterclockwise by a left-handed chef
- Poached Dover sole
- Grass-fed tenderloin with lavender honey
- One pistachio macaron from Ladurée

Background music required: Debussy or Édith Piaf.

Refuses to eat if anyone mispronounces croquette.

House Rules

- Meals must be formally announced:

"Dinner is served, Mademoiselle Farah."

- Tap water is forbidden unless filtered through a Brita blessed by both priest and rabbi.
- No one eats until Mulligan approves the ratios and Farah approves the plating.

Dinner, Without a Shot Fired

Against all odds, dinner was peaceful.

Anna Belle sipped chamomile like an aristocrat.

Teddy demolished ribeye like a cowboy philosopher.

Farah rejected asparagus because it clashed with the placemat.

Mulligan inspected every bowl like a Michelin judge and finally declared,

"Acceptable presentation, Patron."

Julia washed their bowls.

(Yes—crystal.)

Then she looked at me in a way that said, You created this circus.

Just as peace settled over the house, my phone buzzed.

The anxious boy's family had arrived early.

They wondered if our talking service dog could meet him tonight—

before tomorrow's visitation.

Chapter 13 — A Priest, a Rabbi, and a Talking Dog Walk into a Church

Breakfast took an hour to prepare and three minutes to vanish.

Some chefs spend their lives perfecting technique.

Mine happens at 6:10 a.m. with four opinions that bark.

Anna Belle received her poached organic chicken ribbons.

Teddy got steak and eggs—and would've eaten the pan if I'd let him.

Mulligan was served Wagyu medallions in his sacred 62.5/37.5 ratio (don't ask).

And Farah enjoyed a quail-egg omelet whipped counterclockwise by my left hand, because the right hand apparently ruins the texture.

I plated everything like I was auditioning for MasterChef: Funeral Director Edition, and three minutes later, the plates were so clean they could have gone straight back into the cabinet.

While the quartet digested in bliss, I prepped lunch early and prayed they wouldn't notice it would later be reheated in secret.

The Funeral Home Fan Club

We arrived to applause.

Literal applause.

The staff had lined up at the entrance like groupies waiting for a Beatles reunion. Even Larry—formerly known as Fatso—was there, looking noticeably leaner thanks to Mulligan's new "fetch-based cardio regimen."

Once the morning briefing was wrapped, Mulligan, Farah, and I retreated to my office to tackle today's mission:

Convincing my brother—Father Ben—to officiate a dog wedding.

Briefing Mulligan About Father Ben

"Before we get there," I said, "you need to understand Father Ben."

Mulligan sat up, paws crossed, posture of a Jesuit professor.

I ran through the résumé:

- Eagle Scout
- Seminary in Dallas
- Four years in Rome
- Canon Law degree
- Fluent in English, Spanish, Italian (but not Dog French)
- The actual responsible adult in the family

Mulligan nodded thoughtfully.

"I can cover French," he said. "I'm conversational in fourteen dialects of Dog French—two of which I invented."

Of course he was.

Gregorian Howling as Worship

When we reached the parish, the choir was rehearsing Gregorian chant, filling the church with low, ancient echoes.

Farah inhaled.

Mulligan closed his eyes.

Their heads tilted upward.

And then… they joined in.

Perfect harmony.

Perfect pitch.

Gregorian howling.

Father Ben appeared, blinking like he'd just stepped into a theological fever dream.

"Cole," he said slowly, "are those dogs chanting?"

"Technically harmonizing," I said.

He ushered us straight into his office.

I took a breath.

"Ben… Mulligan talks."

Father Ben blinked once.

"May as well go for it," he said. "Mulligan—do your thing."

Mulligan's Vatican Résumé

Mulligan smoothed his imaginary tie, cleared his throat like a professor about to derail a freshman's GPA, and began:

"When I was a pup, I belonged to a man named Jefe—surgeon by day, rabbi by night, amateur magician on weekends."

Father Ben's hand twitched toward his crucifix.

"One day," Mulligan continued, "Jefe and I played golf with the Bishop of Dallas. The Bishop cheated. I corrected his score. He fainted—partly from guilt, mostly from hearing a dog call a penalty."

Father Ben muttered something in Latin that wasn't a blessing.

"So naturally," Mulligan went on, "the Bishop wanted the Pope to meet me. First class to Rome: kosher biscuits, communion wafer for balance."

I closed my eyes.

"But when we landed," Mulligan said, lowering his voice dramatically,

"the Pope had died."

The room went still.

"Staff panicked. Cardinals argued. Swiss Guards dropped their halberds. One fainted. A nun sprained her ankle performing something she called the Urgent Rosary Shuffle. Total chaos."

"And you helped," Father Ben said flatly.

Mulligan nodded. "Father… they needed me."

He began counting on his paw.

"First, I organized the Gentlemen of His Holiness—who, for reasons unknown, were wearing tails longer than mine. I corrected bow depths and insisted on synchronized steps. The Vatican is many things, but synchronized it was not."

Father Ben blinked slowly.

"Second, I advised the papal embalmers. Lovely people, but their cavity-treatment ratios were all wrong. I taught them the sacred 62.5/37.5 rule:

62.5% reverence, 37.5% science—and no cotton rolls bigger than a cannoli."

I choked.

"Third, I supervised the casket preparation. The zinc liner was crooked, the oak dull, and the pall draped like a Motel 6 bedspread. I realigned everything, buffed the lid to within one micron, and centered the papal seal with my muzzle. CNN later called it 'the most symmetrical papal sendoff in modern history.'"

Father Ben was frozen between horror and academic notetaking.

"Fourth, I coordinated liturgical choreography. Deacons kept turning left when the thurifer went right. Incense drifted into the wrong theology. I implemented traffic lanes. Color-coded. Laminated."

He raised his paw solemnly.

"The Church runs on many things, Father—but it should really run on laminated instructions."

"Lord, help me," Father Ben whispered.

I had the feeling we were well past help and into scheduling.

Mulligan continued.

"Fifth, I rewrote the funeral order of service after discovering six misprints, three conflicting responsorial psalms, and one hymn change that could've caused a schism."

"And sixth," he said proudly, "I mediated a dispute between two Cardinals arguing over vestment shades. One insisted on ivory, the other off-white. I reminded them the Pope was colorblind. The matter resolved instantly."

I rubbed my temples.

"At the end," Mulligan said quietly, "a Swiss Guard leaned down and whispered, 'Grazie, Cane Benedetto.'"

Blessed Dog.

Father Ben stared.

"Mulligan," he said at last, "that is completely blasphemous, theologically impossible nonsense."

Mulligan puffed out his chest.

"Thank you, Father. Coming from clergy, that means everything."

⭕ The Ask

"Next Tuesday-ish," I said carefully,

"Mulligan and Farah are getting married.

Mulligan is Jewish.

Farah is Catholic.

We have the rabbi.

We need the Catholic side."

Father Ben looked at the dogs.

Then at me.

Then back at the dogs.

And he grinned.

"Heck yeah," he said. "I wouldn't miss this for anything."

Mulligan pumped his paw.

"I'll draft the vows," he announced. "Interfaith. Interspecies. Entertaining—but reverent."

Father Ben shook his head.

"Cole, you're going straight to confession after this."

"Get in line," I said.

Chapter 14 — Dominoes, Doubts, and Dog Tales

In Which a Club Night Turns Into a TED Talk by a Dog

The Whirlwind Before the Whirlwind

It had been a week.

A French dog trainer fainting.

Mulligan giving a firsthand account of a papal funeral.

A Vatican-adjacent dog wedding now requiring catering, seating charts, and possibly interfaith approval forms.

I hadn't been to the club in days.

My domino buddies had started speculating.

"He joined a monastery."

"He ran away with the French trainer."

"He's taking yoga."

Yoga.

That one hurt.

So I called Julia.

"Mind if I swing by the club?" I asked. "I'll take Mulligan and Farah. Introduce the guys."

She paused.

"Fine. But please, Cole—don't tell them he talks. Let them just be your service dogs tonight."

"Deal," I said.

Which, in hindsight, was blind optimism.

Club Night Begins

On the way over, I glanced in the rearview mirror at the furry Bonnie and Clyde in the back seat.

"Listen," I said. "The club is where I unwind. Drinks, dominoes, trash-talk. Tonight, you two are just well-trained service dogs. No funny stuff."

Mulligan pressed a paw to his chest.

"Scout's honor."

Farah let out a French sigh that said, He says this every time.

As I parked, Julia texted:

Dinner ready when you get home—

Filet mignon cut into golf-ball-sized spheres for Mulligan

Grass-fed tenderloin with lavender honey for Farah

Behave

I assumed that last part applied to all three of us.

The Entrance

The club smelled like laughter, whiskey, and stories older than the furniture.

Then I walked in—with two immaculate "service dogs" who looked like they were about to conduct a board meeting.

Silence.

Not reverent silence.

Suspicious silence.

The men stared like I'd brought pallbearers on leashes.

"Evening, boys," I said. "These are Mulligan and Farah. Newly trained service dogs for the funeral home. Very professional."

A few admired Farah's beauty.

Several others declared Mulligan "the ugliest dog they'd ever seen."

Mulligan gave a low rumble—the canine equivalent of keep talking, Hoss.

I ordered a Cîroc vodka with Topo Chico (no lime), settled into the rhythm of club life, and finally—finally—started to relax.

Then Mulligan tapped my leg.

"What?" I whispered.

He nodded at my drink.

"What about us? We hydrate too."

"Jose?" I said. "Any chance you have Evian?"

He did.

"Two bowls," I clarified.

The bartender delivered them like bottle service in Vegas.

Mulligan nodded, satisfied.

Domino Diplomacy

We migrated to the domino table—

Birdy.

Baylor Boy.

The Dentist.

Buddy the Jewish lawyer.

Urby.

Cameroon.

Mikey the CPA.

Buy-in: ten bucks.

Pride: priceless.

Trash talk: mandatory.

I was mid-hand when Mulligan circled the table like a tournament official, sniffing for strategy. Then he hopped into my lap and pretended to nuzzle me.

"Don't play the double-six," he whispered. "Buddy's holding the double-four."

I nearly swallowed a domino.

"Mulligan," I hissed. "That's cheating."

The table froze.

"You can't tell me Buddy's got the double-four!" I blurted. "And for your information—I already knew that!"

Dead silence.

Mulligan whispered, "Sorry," and hopped down.

Buddy stood, flipped his tiles face-up, and said, "I'm out. I won't play against a mind-reading dog."

So much for being service dogs.

The Reveal

I sighed. "Alright. Full disclosure."

I told them about the Talking Dog—$20 sign.

Told them it wasn't a joke.

Told them he now works for me.

Mulligan hopped onto an empty bar stool, flagged down a whiskey neat with one paw, and gave them his buckle up, boys look.

"Gentlemen," he said, "let me enlighten you."

And then—

MULLIGAN'S LEGENDARY CLUB MONOLOGUE

He cleared his throat like a keynote speaker.

"When I was a pup," he began, "I worked for a man named Jefe—long story, bad hours, paid in bones."

The table leaned in.

"The truth? Jefe was being blackmailed by a cartel. His real name? Jonathan Goldsmith. Rabbi. Surgeon. Motivational speaker. One of the most interesting men alive."

Chuckles.

"He taught me this:

'Mulligan, life is like golf—you never know what's hiding in the rough until you sniff it.'"

Deep man.

They were hooked.

"One spring, Jonathan and I went to Augusta—home of The Masters. I was caddying under an alias: Mulligan Rabinowitz."

Laughter.

"Dogs weren't technically allowed unless you were an emotional-support animal for men in midlife crisis."

The table cracked up.

"We were paired with two Wall Street hotshots and a golf influencer named Lola—heels taller than my vet and a swing like a helicopter accident."

More laughter.

"On the first tee, she bets twenty grand she can out-drive Jonathan. I whisper, 'She tops it.'"

She tops it.

Jonathan wins.

"Next hole, she lines up a putt. I cough—twice—she lips out."

"She screams, 'You HEXED me!'

I said, 'Ma'am, I'm Jewish. We don't do hexes. We do guilt.'"

The place erupted.

"By hole nine, the bets hit a hundred grand and a Bentley. By hole twelve, they were taking tequila shots for bogeys. Nobody remembered the score—except me."

He sipped his whiskey.

"On thirteen, a marshal yelled, 'No dogs on the green!'

I said, 'Buddy, I'm an emotional-support animal for bad decisions.'"

"He waved us on."

The room went quiet.

"Eighteenth hole. A hundred grand on the table.

Jonathan asks, 'Three wood or hybrid?'

I say, 'Neither. I'll hit it.'"

He paused.

"I choke down, waggle, and unleash a 200-yard draw—three feet from the pin."

Gallery gasps.

"Announcer whispers, 'And now…the dog…for birdie.'"

He grinned.

"I rolled it in with my nose. Dead center."

Applause. Laughter. Disbelief.

"Dog Digest gave me a two-page spread. The Golf Channel called it The Most Interesting Round on Earth. Augusta banned me for unsportsmanlike wagging."

He raised a paw.

"And Lola? She told me I ruined her short game but made her year. Next thing I know, I'm judging a bikini-golf charity with her and the Bishop of Dallas. I thought it was for orphans. Turns out Hooters and Tito's sponsored it."

They howled.

"And that, gentlemen," Mulligan concluded, "is why I'm banned from Augusta and an honorary Knight of Columbus. Also—I still have the Bentley."

Silence.

Then someone said, "Bullshit."

Mulligan smiled.

"That's exactly what the crowd said."

He scanned the table.

"Oh—and I remember every one of you who called me ugly. You get one pass tonight."

Next offense?

He bared his teeth.

"I'll bite your ass. Especially you, Rubinski."

The club exploded.

Aftermath

And that was the night Mulligan became a legend at the club—

Beloved in Fort Worth.

Banned in Augusta.

And the only member with both a handicap and a leash.

Chapter 15 — Movie Night and Lime Etiquette

The Return of the Club Champions

When we got home, Mulligan strutted through the front door like a dog who had just delivered a TED Talk on leadership.

Farah glided behind him with effortless grace—if Audrey Hepburn had been an Afghan hound.

Anna Belle and Teddy stood at attention, waiting like Father Ben himself had briefed them.

"Julia," Mulligan announced proudly, "I made new friends tonight. Good men. Strong spirits. Large appetites. But I behaved, Farah behaved, and Patron behaved… in spirit."

Anna Belle inhaled deeply and muttered in doggy English,

"You smell like whiskey and whatever pride smells like."

Teddy offered a translation, also in doggy English:

"Overconfidence mixed with bar snacks."

Mulligan ignored them both.

"And Julia," he continued, "the club served us the finest Evian in Fort Worth. Crisp. Polite. Refined. Farah and I now prefer it with a gentle wisp of lime—four and a half passes. Not five. You never know how well they wash their limes."

Farah nodded once—the continental sign for yes, darling.

Julia stared at him with a look I'd seen many times before.

The one that says: I love you, but you are pushing your luck.

Teddy leaned toward Anna Belle.

"Next he'll ask for lemon wedges shaped like tee markers."

Dinner: A Study in Inequality

Dinner rolled out like a Michelin tasting menu for canines:

- Mulligan: filet mignon rolled into perfect golf-ball spheres
- Farah: grass-fed tenderloin finished in duck fat
- Anna Belle: turkey loaf with a chamomile chaser
- Teddy: bone-in ribeye, because he's Teddy
- Me: leftovers and a spoonful of mashed potatoes

Something about the cosmic balance felt… off.

Afterward, we migrated to the den—me with my laptop, Julia with a blanket, and the dogs forming a seated semicircle like an audience waiting for a magician.

Mulligan Makes a Request

"Patron," Mulligan said, clearing his throat with dignity,

"we'd like to watch a movie tonight."

"You would?" I asked.

"Yes," he said, "and I've prepared a list."

Anna Belle perked up.

"Animated," she said in doggy English. "Make it animated."

Teddy muttered,

"Nothing that makes me cry. Not tonight."

Mulligan nodded, then began.

Mulligan's Top Ten Canine Cinema Picks

1. Hachi: A Dog's Tale (2009)

Stars: Richard Gere

Heart Factor:

"The emotional equivalent of getting hit by a truck made of violins."

2. Marley & Me (2008)

Heart Factor:

"Starts fun. Ends with Julia sobbing into throw pillows."

3. Old Yeller (1957)

Heart Factor:

"A masterpiece. But not tonight. No one is emotionally stable enough."

4. Homeward Bound (1993)

Mood:

"Adventure, loyalty, jokes—everything cinema aims to be."

5. 101 Dalmatians (1961 / 1996)

Couture Rating:

"Cruella De Vil walked so Farah could run."

6. The Call of the Wild (2020)

Mulligan:

"A film for dogs who work out."

7. A Dog's Purpose (2017)

Existential Rating:

"A little deep for a Tuesday."

8. Turner & Hooch (1989)

Laugh Factor:

"Classic chaos."

9. Where the Red Fern Grows (1974)

Warning:

"Not for sensitive adults. Or Teddy."

10. Best in Show (2000)

Laugh Factor:

"Deeply accurate. Painfully so."

Anna Belle dabbed her eyes.

"I can't watch Hachi again."

Teddy growled softly.

"If Old Yeller comes on, I'm walking to Mexico."

The Selection

"So," I asked, "what do you want to watch?"

Mulligan took a breath, looked at Farah tenderly, and said,

"Lady and the Tramp."

"That wasn't even on your list."

"Yeah," he said softly,

"but tonight feels like a romance night."

Farah wagged once.

Anna Belle rolled her eyes.

Teddy sighed.

"Here comes the spaghetti."

Lights, Camera, Canine

We dimmed the lights.

Julia hit play.

Mulligan and Farah curled up like a Hallmark poster.

Anna Belle sprawled across Julia's lap dramatically.

Teddy ate popcorn like he was being paid.

I wondered how this had become my life.

Then the spaghetti scene appeared.

Mulligan whispered,

"That's us, babe."

I threw a pillow at him.

"That's disgusting."

Julia laughed so hard she nearly cried.

Anna Belle muttered,

"You two need professional help."

Teddy added,

"And a second dinner."

Curtain Call

When the credits rolled, Mulligan stretched.

"Patron," he said, "tomorrow we begin wedding planning. Tuesday-ish."

I nodded.

"Of course. Tuesday-ish."

The dogs trotted off—Mulligan proud, Farah elegant, Anna Belle annoyed, Teddy hungry.

I sat in the quiet living room, surrounded by blankets, bowls, and the faint smell of truffle oil.

Talking Dog $20.

One of my better bad decisions.

Chapter 16 — Mulligan the Multilingual Miracle

Breakfast used to be simple.

Not anymore.

Now it involves half a lime,

a bowl of chilled Evian,

and four-and-a-half whiffs waved gently across the surface

like a sommelier blessing water.

According to Mulligan:

Five whiffs meant pretentious.

Four meant amateur hour.

Four-and-a-half meant balance, Patrón — citrus balance.

I tried giving Anna Belle and Teddy tap water once.

They looked at me like I'd brought shame on our ancestors.

Then they started barking rhythmically — organized, unified, and strangely powerful —

like a protest chant:

NO JUSTICE

NO TAP WATER

Our morning walk had evolved into a spectacle.

Mulligan — the grand marshal.

Farah — floating beside him like French couture in motion.

Anna Belle and Teddy — synchronized debutantes with show-dog confidence.

Even Teddy, formerly the neighborhood siren, now walked like a collie who'd discovered therapy.

At the funeral home, Larry stood waiting with a tennis ball in his mouth.

"Larry," I said, "tell me that isn't in your mouth."

He dropped it instantly.

"Just holding it while I text."

Mulligan played fetch with him for thirty straight minutes.

The staff watched like it was the company Olympics.

Larry was shedding pounds.

Mulligan called it core engagement.

I called it odd.

After our meeting, we settled into my office to plan the Tuesday-ish wedding.

Then the phone rang.

A hospice chaplain.

"Cole, I have a family who just moved here from Mexico. Wonderful people. They need someone they can trust."

Within the hour, a stunning family walked in — beautifully dressed, dignified, grief heavy on their faces.

Spanish-speaking only.

I opened Google Translate and fumbled through.

They tried.

I tried.

Grief is heavy.

Words were failing.

Then Mulligan placed his paw gently on my knee and whispered,

"Patrón… déjame hacerlo."

Let me do this.

I looked at him.

The family looked at him.

Even Farah looked at him.

Before anyone could react, Mulligan stepped forward, straightened his imaginary collar, and began speaking.

Not loudly.

Not theatrically.

But with a soft, reverent voice

that filled the room like light.

Mulligan's Speech

"Buenas tardes…"

Good afternoon.

Thank you for allowing me to share this moment with you.

My name is Mulligan — Canine Director of Funeral Services,

and sometimes, a small miracle disguised as a dog.

"Permítanme contarles algo…"

Let me tell you something.

When I was a pup, I lived with a man named Jefe.

People believed he was dangerous.

But I learned he was not evil — only lost.

And in helping him,

I discovered what love really looks like.

"Viajamos por todo México…"

We traveled across Mexico —

through markets that smelled of warm bread and rain,

through plazas where guitars never slept,

through hills where the wind still sings in Spanish.

And everywhere we went, I learned this:

A funeral is not an ending.

It is a thank-you set to music.

"Cuando la mamá de Jefe enfermó…"

When Jefe's mother grew ill with dementia,

I stayed beside her.

At first, I feared she was slipping away.

But one dawn, I saw her laughing softly at the sunrise,

as if she had stepped into a gentler world.

And I understood something important:

Dementia does not steal memories —

it paints them in new colors

the heart can still recognize.

"Por eso estoy aquí…"

That is why I am here now.

Because your mother —

your queen —

deserves a farewell filled with beauty, gratitude,

and the music of a life well-loved.

"Mientras yo respire…"

As long as there is breath in my chest

and shine in my fur,

I will help build a celebration worthy of angels.

"Me llamo Mulligan…"

My name is Mulligan.

And today…

I am part of your family.

Silence.

Beautiful silence — the kind that settles softly on the heart.

Then the eldest son spoke, his voice trembling in the air.

"Se llamaba Rosa Elena Cruz."

My phone translated:

Her name was Rosa Elena Cruz.

A name that carried weight.

A name that carried history.

A name the Spanish-speaking world knew well.

Mulligan inhaled — recognition, not surprise.

"Rosa Elena Cruz…" he repeated softly.

"Ahora… ahora entiendo."

Now… now I understand.

He stepped forward.

The Musical Tribute

"Cuando viajaba por México…"

When I traveled through the sun-drenched villages of Mexico with Jefe, the scent of roasting street corn and the distant strumming of guitars seemed to follow us at every turn.

I heard her.

Everywhere.

In taxis gliding through warm night air.

In kitchens where families sang while they cooked.

In plazas where old couples danced as if time had forgotten them.

"Corazón del Huracán…"

I once heard it played from a balcony in Guanajuato at sunset.

When she hit the high note, even the sky paused to listen.

"Bajo la Misma Luna…"

Jefe hummed it every night he missed his mother.

That song was a prayer disguised as melody.

"Besos de Fuego…"

I once watched a Cantina erupt into joy during that song.

Two men claimed she was singing directly to them.

Neither was sober.

Both felt blessed.

"Reina del Sol…"

Her anthem.

Her crown.

Her light.

When she performed it live in Mexico City,

I swear the earth leaned closer.

He lifted his eyes to the family.

"Your mother was not just a star.

She was a soundtrack.

A memory that belonged to millions —

but was born in your home."

The family broke.

Softly.

Beautifully.

They embraced him —

tears falling into his fur like blessings.

The Dignitaries & the Dream Service

After that, planning flowed like sacred water.

Names emerged.

Cardinal Esteban de la Vega — whose sermons could move stone to tears.

Paloma del Río — the national voice of heartbreak and hope.

Don Rafael Castillo-Ortiz — philanthropist and patron of the arts.

Dr. Lucía Herrera Cortés — Poet Laureate of Mexico.

This was not just a funeral.

It was a farewell for a queen.

Bass Hall.

A multilingual program in seven languages.

A gold-plated casket with an azure interior.

Two hundred musicians.

Three hundred singers.

Flowers enough to perfume heaven.

Mulligan coordinated it all

as though he had been born for this moment.

When the family finally left,

their faces were lighter,

their grief gentler.

I looked down at Mulligan.

He straightened his invisible tie.

"Good boy, Mulligan," I whispered.

He answered softly, with humility that felt holy:

"Just doing God's work, Patrón."

Talking Dog $20.

Sometimes the miracle isn't that the dog talks —

but that he speaks directly

to the places inside us

that need healing the most.

Chapter 17 — Floral Budgets and Other Miracles

I hugged Mulligan like a long-lost son.

I have a great son — Luke — but Mulligan had just sold the greatest funeral I may ever conduct. In that moment, he wore the expression of someone who had passed the bar exam, conquered Everest, and negotiated Middle East peace before breakfast.

Today, together, we hadn't just arranged a funeral.

We had arranged the funeral.

The kind they'll whisper about in boardrooms, barbershops, and back pews until the end of Texas time.

I took a long breath.

"Buddy… your Tuesday-ish wedding is now officially… more ish."

Mulligan froze.

Farah wilted like a French supermodel hearing the word buffet.

"Welcome to the funeral business," I told him. "I once left the hospital where Luke had just been born. I saw him placed in the nursery — and then I had to rush off to handle a service.

This is how it goes."

Mulligan nodded solemnly, his eyes softening.

"Patrón," he said, "I told them they were my family. I understand. Anyway… I think Farah will keep loving me."

Farah, to her credit, nodded once with regal restraint.

I, however, was already imagining the guest list:

- Half runway hounds with owners in pink brocade

- Half cartel canines in tuxedos

• And us in the middle, praying OSHA didn't show up

A wedding and a state-level funeral back-to-back.

This wasn't work — this was cardio disguised as grief care.

Casket — CHECK

The gold-plated casket with the azure-blue velvet interior.

I called the manufacturer.

They answered the phone like I'd just announced free donuts.

"That one? The gold one? Yes, sir! Immediately! Right away! Shall we deliver it with a parade?"

By the tone of their voice, they were already stitching

THANK YOU, FORT WORTH

into a commemorative banner.

A private jet would deliver it the next afternoon.

Casket — done.

Cemetery — CHECK

Next, I called the cemetery superintendent.

This is a man who has rearranged bushes, benches, and once an entire water feature for a family who wanted "more ambiance."

I explained the Cruz needs:

• A newly platted section

• Fountains

• Benches

• Walkways

• Possibly an amphitheater

He didn't miss a beat.

"We'll reroute a few hedges and a small chapel and get it ready."

A chapel.

Like it was a potted fern.

Cemetery — done.

Funeral Bulletin — CHECK

Thirty pages.

Multilingual.

Paper so fine it could double as Vatican stationery.

I called the printer.

"Think wedding invitation meets papal decree," I said.

He didn't ask why.

He whispered, reverently,

"I'll start the presses."

Bulletin — done.

Florals — and This Is Where the Lord Tests Us

While I sorted logistics, Mulligan contacted the florist.

I overheard him give an email address.

"mulligan@csfuneral.com"

I blinked.

"Was that the florist?"

"Yes, Patrón. They'll send ideas and pricing shortly."

Ideas and pricing.

Two words that chill the bones of any seasoned funeral director.

Moments later, my computer chimed.

I opened the PDF and said words that should never be spoken in front of polite company or clergy.

The Floral Estimate of Destiny

Estimated Cost Breakdown — "Celebration of Life"

Entrance of Angels Archway

Oaxacan tuberoses, phantom orchids, Thai moon orchids dusted in gold, vines, pearls, scaffolding

$97,000

Garden of Remembrance Aisle

Marigolds, blue roses, Himalayan black orchids, lighting crew

$29,500

Altar of Memory Display

Ecuadorian roses, Casablanca lilies, proteas, carved onyx urn vases

$43,500

Celebration Canopy Reception

Kyoto peonies, tropicals, 3,000 orchids, scent diffusers, rigging crew

$75,000

Farewell Bouquet (Casket Piece)

500 white roses + NASA-approved gold stardust

$8,000

Post-Funeral Fiesta Centerpieces

40 altar pieces, 120 keepsake orchids

$13,000

Logistics & Handling

Customs, reefers, international freight, floral insurance

$39,500

GRAND TOTAL: $305,500

(give or take a bouquet)

I stared at the number.

"Mulligan," I called, "your twenty-five-thousand-dollar floral budget may be a little… optimistic."

He padded over, read the total—

—and wagged his tail.

WAGGED.

HIS.

TAIL.

"I'll email the coordinator," he said calmly. "I'll tell them this is what could be done, and they may choose what they like."

He typed:

If Heaven had a front door, this would be it — and we just rented it for the weekend.

Within minutes, the reply came back:

Perfect. We'll take it all.

Mulligan turned to me, eyes shining with celestial mischief.

"Patrón… sometimes you have to think celestial."

Talking Dog $20.

At this rate, I'm not just planning a funeral.

I'm planning my own canonization.

$20

At this rate, I'm not just planning a funeral.

I'm planning my own canonization.

Chapter 18 — The Table Knows

I almost swung by the club.

Almost.

One quick drink, I told myself.

Thirty minutes of questionable wisdom from men who have never been wrong in their own memories.

But the day had been too big—

Bass Hall, a gold-plated casket arriving by private jet,

the Cruz family, Mulligan becoming the Mexican Churchill—

and my adrenaline collapsed so fast I felt it in my knees.

In the back seat, Mulligan and Farah slept curled together,

like two French poets whispering Dog French lullabies.

I pointed the car toward home.

Halfway down Camp Bowie, I remembered—I had not spoken to Luke.

Not once.

I hit call.

Luke answered immediately.

"You're not going to believe the funeral I arranged today," I said.

That woke Mulligan right up.

"The funeral you arranged?" he barked from the back seat.

I waved the universal not now sign and kept talking.

Mrs. Cruz. Bass Hall. Bilingual programs.

Dignitaries stacked like cordwood.

Three hundred thousand dollars in florals.

"Dad... that's incredible," Luke said.

"And if you want the full version," I added,

"Come over Saturday. Bring Annette, Arnold, Newton John... and Jack the Jack Russell. He'll love the chaos."

We hung up as I pulled into the driveway.

"So," Mulligan said, "no credit for orchestrating the greatest funeral in modern history?"

"You get the credit," I told him. "It's just easier to explain in person."

The House and the Weight

Inside, Anna Belle and Teddy greeted us like a ticker-tape parade for people who smell like Cheez-Its and car upholstery.

We walked straight into Julia's quiet storm.

Four cutting boards.

Eight pans.

Steam rising like disciplined incense.

Dinner was organized into quadrants:

- Mulligan — steak cubes, jeweler-perfect
- Farah — salmon, parsley, a rice tower approaching Eiffel height
- Anna Belle — chicken and sweet potato in military-precision dice
- Teddy — lean beef and green beans in golf-ball portions

Ninety minutes of my breakfast had taken her one hundred fifty minutes for dinner.

And she was wilted.

I started telling her about the Cruz family—private jets, orchestras, florals—and she did not turn.

Didn't blink.

Didn't murmur.

She just kept working, quietly drowning in devotion.

"Hey," I said softly.

"I love them," she whispered. "I really do. I'd do anything for them.

I'm just... not sure I can keep this up."

Something broke in me.

"Mulligan," I murmured, "take everyone outside. Ten minutes. Come back through the dog door."

He nodded and herded the dogs out like a furry usher staff.

The Work of Two Tired Hearts

I poured Julia a drink.

Poured myself one.

I stationed myself at Farah's quadrant and began slicing filets into tiny Pro V1s.

Two exhausted people—

stacking rice towers,

garnishing parsley,

trying to fix something bigger than dinner.

"When we leave," Julia whispered,

"I have four dog beds to change. Fresh sheets every day. Because Mulligan insists."

"You can't buy dog-bed sheets, Cole. I had to sew them.

He told me I left a thread."

I wanted to laugh.

I did not.

We plated dinner and carried everything into the dining room.

And that is when the table took over.

The Table That Remembers

Hand-carved mahogany by Eli Rosenfeld—

a Greenwich Village artist who read Whitman aloud while sanding.

He refused nails. Called them interruptions to the conversation.

He hid a small brass compass rose beneath the table apron so diners would always know where home was.

Only a dozen Rosenfeld tables exist.

Ours had survived five decades of roast beef, report cards, and my father carving brisket like scripture.

Tonight, it held:

- A Michelin tasting menu for a talking dog

- His Afghan bride

- Their siblings

- And two people trying not to drown

Julia at one end.

Me at the other.

Dogs sitting like diplomats.

The air was thin.

Everyone felt the wobble.

The Soft Collapse

After dinner, Julia sat on the couch and stared at the wall.

Mulligan climbed up beside her.

Farah, Anna Belle, and Teddy gathered at her feet.

He placed a paw gently on her wrist.

"I'm sorry," he said quietly.

No flourish.

No ego.

Just truth.

"I think I have asked too much."

Julia didn't move.

"You need to know something," he continued.

"In these few days… we already loved you. You made us feel home."

He looked at Teddy.

"Teddy told us he was sick and scared when he arrived—nobody's first pick.

But you loved him instantly."

A tear slid down Julia's cheek.

"And Anna Belle," he added,

"Says she wants to call you Jan… because it makes her feel like she belongs."

Julia's shoulders softened.

"So we made a plan," Mulligan said. "Farah thought of it first."

"We Googled personal chefs. We hired one. She starts tomorrow."

Julia blinked. "You did what?"

"And we're interviewing housekeepers," Mulligan added proudly.

"You don't have money," she said.

"Patrón will pay us eventually," he replied.

"We're salaried staff. Partially compensated in brisket."

Her mouth almost twitched into a smile.

"What's her name?"

"Eliana," Mulligan said.

"She cooks in honor of the man who made your table.

Food should respect the wood that carries it."

The table hummed, as if approving.

Julia let out a long, tired breath.

"I don't need a Michelin circus," she whispered.

"I just need help."

"And now," Mulligan said,

"You have it."

The dogs pressed into her in a silent vow.

No schedules.

No budgets.

Just home.

The Compass Rose

Hours later, the house quiet, I brushed my hand beneath the table edge and found the tiny brass compass rose.

Pointing north.

Always north.

"Tomorrow," I whispered, "we feed the house."

And behind me, a talking dog kept watch in the quiet—

without saying a word.

Chapter 19 — The Chef, the Casket, and the Confession

That morning, breakfast took one hour and forty-five minutes.

By minute fifteen, I questioned my sanity.

By minute forty-five, I questioned my theology.

By minute sixty-five, I questioned where my life had gone wrong.

Some men cook to relax.

I cook because four dogs have standards that make Michelin inspectors look sloppy.

Anna Belle's poached ribbons.

Teddy's steak and eggs, seared like a cowboy's memory.

Mulligan's sacred 665/335 Wagyu ratio.

Farah's quail-egg omelet whisked counterclockwise.

("For texture, Patrón—texture.")

So when I remembered our new personal chef was arriving that day, I nearly fell to my knees.

If ever there was a time to hang up the apron, this was it.

The Funeral Home, and Fatso the Labrador-in-Training

When we pulled into the funeral home, I found Fatso—Larry—on all fours in the parking lot, tennis ball in mouth, tail wagging hard enough to power a ceiling fan.

I stared.

I needed caffeine too badly to intervene.

A tennis ball shot past my ankle.

Fatso bounded after it with joyful, Labrador-like abandon.

"Oh dear Lord," I muttered.

"He's not even embarrassed anymore."

And somehow, he looked slimmer.

Turns out fetch-based cardio works—

even when your trainer is a talking dog with a whistle complex.

Paperwork, Wedding Plans, and One Serious Confession

I was in my office reviewing Cruz service paperwork when Mulligan and Farah entered like they owned equity in the funeral home.

"Mulligan," I said, "what you told Julia last night... she needed that. Thank you."

"We love her, Cole. She's the greatest."

"And how exactly did you hire the chef?" I asked.

He grinned innocently, always a bad sign.

"Well... you hired her. She thinks she was talking to you."

I put my head on the desk.

"Oh. Swell. Perfect."

"And yes," he added cheerfully, "I told her she'd be on a private jet."

I looked up.

"I didn't not tell her about the casket."

"Wonderful," I groaned.

"Nothing says 'welcome to the team' like an airborne sarcophagus."

"And" he continued, "Farah and I want the wedding the day after the funeral. The coordinator says we can reuse some of the flowers."

I blinked.

"You what?"

Then came the final blow.

"…and we want Paloma del Río to sing Reina del Sol—live."

"Mulligan," I said, "this is a funeral home, not a telenovela."

He shrugged.

"Some say a wedding feels like a funeral anyway."

The Plane, the Panic, the Chef

The day blurred—calls, confirmations, quartets, logistics.

Then the call came.

The plane was thirty minutes out.

On the runway, the jet door opened—

and our new chef descended like a Hitchcock heroine who had just escaped a villain.

She was pale.

Wild-eyed.

Breathless.

"You know I just sat next to a casket for two hours?!" she cried.

"I thought I was being kidnapped. Or murdered. Or both!"

"Oh no, no," I said quickly.

"It's empty. Completely empty."

I glared at Mulligan.

He shrugged.

"I figured since the plane was available, she wouldn't mind sharing the ride."

Eliana exhaled so hard my hair moved.

"And you're… not here to murder me," she said slowly,

"and did that dog just speak?"

"Of course not," I smiled.

"But let's continue this conversation somewhere with fewer dead props."

The Ride Back, the Truth, and the Reveal

I decided honesty was the only way forward.

"Okay… it wasn't me who called you.

It was Mulligan."

She stared.

"The dog?"

"Technically, yes."

I explained everything—the century-old funeral home, Señora Cruz, the upcoming canine wedding, and Julia's desperate need for help.

She listened quietly, then asked,

"You really think I'm the right one?"

"I do," I said. "More than you know."

Her shoulders dropped.

"Okay," she said. "Then what about the dog?"

Mulligan cleared his throat—a tiny, theatrical hem-hem—sat upright in the Sprinter like a furry diplomat summoned before the UN, and began.

"Chef Eliana… allow me to introduce myself properly.

"My name is Mulligan.

And yes—I'm a talking dog."

He paused.

Farah angled herself like his personal publicist.

"When I was a pup, I belonged to a man named Jefe—a cartel boss of questionable morals and impeccable taste in leather sofas. He discovered early on that I could talk and used me to spy on his men. I'd lie under the conference table, pretending to nap, listening to betrayal, skimming, and one inexplicable argument about cilantro."

His voice dropped.

"One night, everything went wrong. Bullets. Sirens. Someone shouting, 'WHO BOUGHT THE WRONG CILANTRO!' In the chaos, I ran. I ran until my paws hit a golf course. And there—under a moonlit bunker—I met the ghost of Ben Hogan."

He lifted a paw heavenward.

"Ben taught me discipline, posture, and the importance of a firm back paw. But more importantly, he said, 'Mulligan… crime and golf aren't your destiny. Culture is.'"

Eliana blinked.

Mulligan continued.

"So I left cartel life behind and rebranded myself as The Most Interesting Dog in the World. Since then, I've:

- dined with presidents

- out-drunk Hemingway's ghost in Key West

- once convinced Gordon Ramsay to apologize to a soufflé

- judged Iron Chef blindfolded and wrote my notes in iambic pentameter

- invented farm-to-table cuisine before humans caught on

- served as spiritual caddy to Ben Hogan's ghost

- written a memoir—Mulligan: The Taste of Danger—banned in three countries for revealing state secrets, and one for revealing the Colonel's secret recipe

"Anthony Bourdain said I had 'the palate of a saint and the table manners of a pirate.'

"I took that as a compliment."

He shifted, tail swishing with dignified pride.

"I have cooked in Paris, plated in Tokyo, garnished in Milan, and sautéed under fire—literally. I once performed a tableside flambé during a hostage negotiation."

Farah nodded like she had been there.

"And now…"

His voice softened.

"…now I am humbled—truly humbled—to stand beside a chef of your caliber.

"I'm told your risotto makes grown men weep.

Your béchamel has saved marriages.

Your tamales have ended wars.

Your crema has caused fistfights in the Vatican."

Eliana's mouth fell open in a half-laugh, half-gasp.

"So together, Chef Eliana, we will create meals so exquisite the angels of the Rainbow Bridge will weep with hunger.

"Duck confit for dogs.

Filet mignon for guests.

And an amuse-bouche so powerful it could raise the dead—which, in my line of work, would greatly complicate things."

He sat back, proud and serene.

"Anyway," he concluded gently,

"I've lived a life—cartels, cuisine, chaos.

But today, Chef…

"I am simply a humble dog.

Ready for dinner."

The Sprinter went silent.

Eliana stared at him for a full five seconds, then said,

"That has got to be the biggest load of bullshit I have ever heard."

Then she smiled—big, bright, and real.

"But put me in, Coach.

"I'm a yes."

Chapter 20 — Gold on Gold (and a Chef)

By the time we rolled back from the airport, one gold-plated casket in tow, plus my newly acquired, possibly gold-plated chef—I felt like I was driving a Brinks truck with better manners.

It seemed only right to introduce Chef Eliana Duarte to the Sheridan crew, walk the building, and align us for our upcoming double-header:

The Farewell of the Century

and

A Dog Wedding Drifting from Tuesday-ish to Gloriously Ish

Larry's Grand Entrance

At the front door stood Larry—formerly "Fatso," in our less charitable era—on all fours with a tennis ball in his mouth and a brand-new Hollywood Feed collar. The tags were still dangling, like the price label on a tux in a sitcom.

"You left the tags on, Larry," I said. "Now be a good boy and go back to your office."

Eliana raised an eyebrow.

I shrugged. "He's taking the whole 'talking dog' situation surprisingly well."

Touring the Kingdom

I walked her through the chapel, the family rooms, and finally the reception hall and kitchen—our stainless-steel pride and joy.

She lingered there in profound, chefly silence.

The kind that translates to: Yes. Yes. This temple will do nicely.

Combi ovens that could moonlight at the Ritz tend to have that effect.

Back in my office, we sat—me, Eliana, Mulligan, and Farah—like a board meeting where only two participants were technically human.

The coordinator had texted Mulligan (not me, naturally):

• Calling hours would rotate food every fifteen minutes for eight straight hours

• A parking-lot spotter would count arrivals

• Every guest would be met at the door with a white, red, and champagne tray—one glass per guest, poured immediately

If you decline wine?

Too bad. Mulligan's theology insists wine goes stale as fast as Evian.

Then came the line that should have come with a defibrillator:

"Keep wines reasonable. Nothing over $500 a bottle. Reception budget may be... broader."

I glanced at Eliana.

"First course of business," I said—then paused, grinning. "Course."

Nothing.

Tough room.

Then I handed her my laminated dog menu like a father presenting ultrasound photos.

"You're going to be impressed."

She smiled faintly when someone suggested microwaving béarnaise.

"I'll have something ready," she said.

Arrival & Walkthrough

When we returned two hours later, my office had transformed into some kind of culinary Hogwarts.

On my desk rested three leather-bound books—engraved, hand-lettered, and reverent—like Eliana had moonlighted as a monk in a nineteenth-century monastery.

Mulligan placed a paw on the stack.

Farah tilted her head like a duchess evaluating a new opera house.

Eliana gestured.

"Shall we?"

The Calling Hours, Champagne Hours... All the Hours

"The coordinator's cadence works beautifully," she said. "Two refined bites and a two-ounce pour every fifteen minutes, under the $500 cap."

Mulligan nodded sagely—like a bishop approving scripture he'd secretly ghostwritten.

The Leather Books (and a Small Coronary)

First Book: The Reception

The Farewell of the Century — For Rosa Elena Cruz

A twilight hacienda draped in candles.

White roses laced with marigolds.

A string quartet dissolving into mariachi.

Food bending time and reason.

The Champagne Prelude — To the Light

- Salon Blanc de Blancs 2013
- Gold-leafed oyster
- Osetra on avocado mousse
- Micro-empanadas with truffle and foie gras

Then came five Imperial Stations—Puebla, Garden, Ocean, Ranch, and Angels—each paired with wines so expensive the bottles should have come with armed security.

Estimated Budget: ~$107,000

Eliana's note, hand-inked beneath:

May every guest leave saying, "I've never tasted grief this beautifully."

Mulligan dabbed his eyes.

Farah blinked, as if protecting invisible mascara.

Second Book: The Calling Hours

Thirty-two rotations.

Eight hours.

Two bites.

Two-ounce pours.

Hourly floral refreshes.

Representative samples:

- Short-rib crostini

- Ceviche spoons

- Lavender shortbread crosses

Estimated Budget: ~$73,000

Closer:

Grief and gratitude share the same table.

Mulligan whispered,

"Put that on a wall."

Third Book: The House-Dog Menu

The Sheridan Family Canine Culinary Program

Hand-lettered like scripture.

Served at 101°F.

Evian allowed to "breathe."

Weekly menus included:

- Anna Belle — Delicate Flower with Cast-Iron Bark
- Teddy — Red-Meat Texan Thunder
- Mulligan — Precision Palate of a Golf-Course Spy
- Farah — Runway Muse of Versailles

Rules included:

- Formal announcements
- Blessed Brita water
- Plating approval by Farah
- Ratio approval by Mulligan
- No repetition (culinary malpractice)

Weekly dog-food budget: ~$575

I refused eye contact with my wallet.

Decision, Delight, and Damage to Wallet

Mulligan closed the third book with ceremony.

"Patrón," he breathed, "we have found our chef."

I groaned into the ceiling.

"Talking Dog—twenty dollars, and there goes my canonization."

Eliana bowed to Farah, shook Mulligan's paw, and officially took her place in our household food chain.

Just then, my phone buzzed:

- Casket wheels down at 9 a.m.
- Florist at dawn

- Father Ben: Bring the dog
- Mulligan mouthed: Rehearsal dinner

Chapter 21 — Sidecar Diplomacy

The car ride home had a strange soundtrack:

half poetry, half purring, half… French.

Or rather, Dog French—which, as Mulligan is quick to remind you, is a vastly different dialect from anything spoken in Paris.

Eliana glanced back at the dogs, eyebrows raised.

"That's an unusual sound for dogs."

"That's Doggy French," I said.

"Dog French," Mulligan corrected,

with the clipped authority of a Parisian maître d' rejecting the soup.

Farah added a soft, operatic trill.

Mulligan followed with a deep-baritone hum.

Two furry French diplomats, mid–cultural exchange.

Then Mulligan tapped my shoulder.

"Patrón, administrative note:

We promised Mom—

(we know you said 'Jules,' but we prefer 'Mom')—

that we'd secure a maid and nanny.

I've compiled résumés, references, background checks, and two shortlists."

"We'll look at them later," I said.

"Tomorrow I'm playing golf."

"Perfect," he replied. "I'll play."

"No, you will not."

"Then I'll ride."

"Absolutely not."

"Does this vehicle have a trailer hitch?"

"No."

"The hearse?"

"Casket coach. Still no."

"The Suburban?"

"…At the funeral home."

Mulligan smiled—

the kind of smile that means a plan has been made

and a check has already cleared.

"Excellent. My golf-cart sidecar was delivered there.

Slightly used.

Had your accountant overnight the check."

I didn't ask how much.

I was conserving strength.

Evening Calm (Mostly)

Eliana cooked with the kind of casual brilliance

that makes you question every decision you've ever made in a kitchen.

Julia and I ate like two commoners

who had accidentally wandered into Versailles.

Ten minutes into a Lassie rerun, the humans were asleep.

The dogs were riveted.

Lassie is basically CNN for them.

Morning Ritual: Dress Code for Canine Golfers

I came downstairs in a regular golf shirt.

Mulligan descended like he was walking onto Augusta—

custom Ben Hogan cap, chest out, stride purposefully.

Farah followed like Audrey Hepburn on her way to brunch in Saint-Tropez—

silk scarf, perfect posture, zero apology.

We swung by the funeral home.

Larry met us at the door, hopeful.

When I told him we were "just grabbing the Suburban,"

Larry deflated like a parade balloon left out in July.

Poor guy.

He just wants to be part of the mission.

The Sidecar, the Crowd, and the Consequences

When we arrived at Ridglea Country Club,

Mulligan's new sidecar caused a commotion.

A crowd gathered—

amused, astonished, confused,

and generously ribbing.

Ben Rubinski was already on the first tee.

"No shenanigans," I warned.

"Of course," Mulligan said.

(Which is dog code for prepare for shenanigans.)

Hole One

On Ben's backswing,

Mulligan whistled a slow, tragic funeral dirge.

Ben nearly whiffed it.

"That's enough," I snapped.

"It's a funeral tune, Patrón," Mulligan whispered.

"For his opening drive."

Hole Three

Ben set his cigar down to swing.

Mulligan calmly trotted over…

lifted a leg…

and relieved himself on the end of it.

Ben picked the cigar up.

Stuck it back in his mouth.

Chewed.

Paused.

Then made the face of a man

who'd licked a nine-volt battery

wrapped in lemons.

"MULLIGAN!"

He froze.

"Understood," he said. "We'll be quiet."

To their credit, they behaved for the rest of the round—

except when I hit a decent shot

and they howled, circled the cart,

and performed what I believe was a victory samba.

Barstool Diplomacy

(Also known as the moment I nearly lost my membership)

We finished, settled bets,

and—like civilized men—ordered drinks.

I stepped away for three minutes.

When I returned through the heavy oak doors,

Mulligan had taken over the Ridglea Men's Club.

He sat on a barstool like a minor duke.

Farah perched beside him with a glass of Evian

and a single olive—because of course she did.

Mulligan had something amber in front of him.

I didn't ask.

I didn't want to know.

The old guard—cigars, stories, and statins—

was locked in.

"Gentlemen," Mulligan was saying,

paw resting on the bar like he owned equity,

"I've been studying human behavior.

Not an expert, mind you—

though after observing this group,

I may be the closest thing you've got."

I walked in on:

- "Some men can't meet new people without sniffing around first.

I say shake hands, not tails—it's cleaner."

- "I told Larry last week you can't chase every car that passes.

He said, 'How else do you get promoted in this town?'

Explains the tire marks on his résumé."

- "My neighbor's dating life reminds me of a fire hydrant—

everyone stops by, no one stays long."

• "They say money can't buy happiness. True.

But it can buy a leather chair, a sunbeam,

and quiet from two to four in the afternoon.

That's all I require."

• "You can always tell the alpha in a marriage.

It's the one who gets fed first

and still pretends to wait for the other."

• "Someone asked if I'd ever been neutered.

I said, 'Sir, I've been married. Does that count?'"

• "You ever notice how some men wag when the boss walks in?

In my day, we called that networking."

• "My doctor told me to stop burying my problems.

Where else am I supposed to put them—under the porch?"

• "I don't chase cars anymore.

Now I lease them. Easier on the joints."

He finished with a languid curl of his tail around the barstool leg,

glanced at Farah,

and took a tiny, scandalous sip of his not-water.

Homeward, with Only Mild Felonies

On the way home, Mulligan stretched out in the back seat.

"A successful outing," he said.

"Minimal shenanigans."

"Minimal?" I repeated.

He nodded proudly.

"Patrón… I like Mom's house.

And I like your club."

Something warm settled in my chest.

"Good," I said. "Let's try to keep both."

"Tomorrow," he added,

"we revisit the maid and nanny candidates.

I've ranked them by temperament, vacuum competency,

and accent."

"Accent?"

"Preferably French.

Dog French uptake will be faster."

We still had a state funeral to plan,

a wedding to delay,

and a chef who had reorganized my entire life.

But we made it home.

Barely.

Chapter 22 — The Doctor, the Diet, and the Dying Appetite

By this point in my life, I should have recognized the pattern:

whenever a new "helper" entered our household, my life expectancy didn't decrease medically—

just emotionally.

…and spiritually.

When I walked downstairs and found all four dogs seated formally at my parents' dining table—

speaking polite Dog English while Farah demanded Dog French translation—

I knew one thing:

Today was going to hurt me.

Continental Breakfast, Canine Edition

The dogs sat upright in high-backed chairs.

China place settings.

Linen napkins.

Posture fit for ambassadors—

or criminals pretending innocence.

Teddy laughed in French.

I apologized silently to my parents' furniture.

I slipped toward the kitchen, hoping for biscuits, bacon,

and a gravy boat large enough to swim laps in.

Instead, I got Eliana.

A Chef's Diagnosis

She stood at the counter like a physician about to deliver news gently—

but not that gently.

My prescription bottles were lined up beside her,

like jurors already leaning toward conviction.

"Cole," she said,

"you are carrying too much… packaging."

Then came the inspection.

Waist.

Chin.

Soul.

"Before I was a chef," she said,

"I was a doctor.

Before I was a doctor, I was a pharmacist.

Before that…"

she paused,

"I created medicine."

From behind her, Mulligan whispered helpfully,

"Maybe start with his cholesterol."

Eliana lifted each bottle in turn.

"Blood pressure."

"Stomach."

"Heart."

"Peeing."

Then she looked at me—kind, direct, mercilessly.

"Patrón… you take medicine for everything

except joy."

I began to defend myself.

She was not impressed.

The Healing Menu (With Emotional Damage)

She read my new diet like a sentencing order.

Breakfast:

Warm lemon water.

One dry corner of toast.

One almond.

"One almond?" I asked.

Mulligan nodded.

"Cruel but fair."

Lunch:

Kale.

Chia.

Shame.

Dinner:

Steamed broccoli.

One tofu cube.

A whiff of grilled chicken.

No coffee.

No wine.

No sweet tea—

"a crime against the pancreas."

My Southern blood cried out in protest.

Julia's Counter-Prescription (Mercy in Human Form)

Then Julia walked in.

And suddenly, Eliana softened.

Julia's menu included:

- Pomegranate juice
- Goat-cheese omelet
- Sourdough with French butter
- Pistachio-crusted salmon
- Dark-chocolate mousse

Mine?

A celery stick.

And a mindful moment.

I have never hated a vegetable more.

Residency Requirements (and Rituals I Did Not Approve)

Eliana announced that the guest house would require:

- New flooring
- Skylights
- Soundproofing "for evening rituals"

I did not ask.

Mulligan leaned toward me and whispered,

"If the universe talks back, we're moving."

She then outlined her morning practice:

Sunrise Fusion Flow Yoga

with Interpretive Barking.

Farah approved immediately, of course.

Tools of the Trade — and the Black Card

Next came the kitchen upgrades.

Copper cookware.

Himalayan salt blocks.

A Pyrenees monk mortar.

Herbal distillers.

Something involving smoke, prayer, and intention.

Then she held out her hand.

"For your card."

I handed it over.

She stared.

She gasped.

She lifted it as if she had drawn Excalibur from the stone.

"A Black Card," she whispered reverently.

"Patrón… the culinary heavens have opened."

She spun away, humming

what sounded like a Gregorian-salsa hybrid.

Mulligan sighed.

"You just armed a magician with unlimited credit."

And he wasn't wrong.

The Italian Invasion

Some chapters are chaotic. Some chapters are spiritual
And some chapters… introduce an Italian maid-nanny
who may or mamot be sanctioned by the Vatican

- ✓ A floral-scarf runway model (Farah)
- ✓ A debonair troublemaker in a Hogan cap (Mulligan)
- ✓ Larry is attempting interpretive concrete art
- ✓ A résumé so Italien it should come with subtitles
- ✓ And the arrival of a maid-nanny who wears Chanel to mop

Chapter 23 — The Italian Invasion

Eliana drove off in a cloud of perfume so thick the EPA could've gotten involved. As her taillights disappeared, I swear I heard a mashup of Ave Maria and salsa lingering in the air behind her. Only Eliana could leave a driveway smelling like a cathedral and a Cuban nightclub at the same time.

I swallowed the last imaginary bite of biscuits and gravy—the only breakfast I'm allowed to enjoy now. Mulligan cleaned his paws like a brunch critic. Farah adjusted her silk scarf as though she'd survived a mild inconvenience rather than the Category 5 Chihuahua incident earlier that morning.

"All right," I said. "Let's get to work."

"We are not ready," Mulligan announced.

"You don't shower. You don't change clothes. You don't brush your teeth," I said.

He froze, lifted one paw with wounded dignity, and whispered,

"Patrón... if I only had hands."

Two minutes later, I heard it clacking.

They returned dressed like they had stepped off a private jet:

• Mulligan, in his Hogan cap, worn like a debonair caddy-slash–Italian film star

• Farah, in a floral silk scarf so dramatic it could have closed Milan Fashion Week

"Mulligan," I said, "we are not playing golf today."

"I know," he said, tipping the brim. "But I look debonair. And Farah... she is radiant."

Farah executed a slow runway turn. She glowed like a supermodel filming a fragrance commercial titled Chanel No Good Girl.

Administrative Notes, Dog Edition

Halfway down Camp Bowie, Mulligan cleared his throat—the sound he makes right before something expensive happens.

"Patrón, you have a two o'clock."

"With whom?"

"Our new maid-slash-nanny. I invited her. She accepted. She is perfect."

"You… invited… someone… to my office?"

He puffed up like a rooster in a designer vest.

"Brand management, Patrón. Also—she only speaks Italian."

"WE don't speak Italian!"

"I am fluent," he said proudly. "I oversaw the Pope's funeral. And I read Italian for Dummies. It is Spanish with passion and hand gestures. Bellissimo."

I prayed silently.

Parking-Lot Pupdates

We pulled into the lot, where Larry lay on his back making concrete snow angels while humming Who Let the Dogs Out like a Gregorian chant.

"LARRY!" I yelled.

He scrambled up with such enthusiasm that gravity briefly considered resigning.

"Can we play today?" he asked, presenting a soggy tennis ball like the Crown Jewels.

Inside, Fa leaned over her desk.

"He says he's lost 150 pounds," she whispered.

"In dog pounds."

I rubbed my eyes.

"Sadly… believable."

Thirty minutes later, Mulligan and Farah glided in, smug.

"Larry is improving," Mulligan reported. "We are calling him Notsofatso."

"Whatever helps him sleep."

Hey, Sorry — The Voice Assistant We Actually Need

"You should use the office voice systems," Mulligan said. "You never talk to them."

"They don't understand me," I said. "I need a Southern one. I'd call her Sorry."

"Sorry?" he asked.

"Yeah. Like—

'Hey, Sorry, I'm starvin"

She says: 'Whatcha want?'

I say: 'Mezkin.'

She says: 'Fuel City. Four tacos. Extra sauce. Don't let 'em cheat you. And get street corn from the lady outside.'

Then she gives directions using landmarks that closed ten years ago and tells me to ignore the Trucks Only sign."

Mulligan nodded.

"You just invented redneck GPS."

"The world's not ready," I said.

THE RÉSUMÉ

Candidate: Signora Bella Fiorella di Lucca

Maid. Nanny. Domestic Revolutionary. Possibly canonized.

Mulligan slid the résumé across my desk like a mafia confession.

Résumé Highlights

(Translated. Lightly Sanitized. Spiritually Dangerous.)

Name:

Signora Bella Fiorella di Lucca, DOC

(Designata Onoraria della Canine Cultura — Honorary Designer of Canine Culture)

Languages:

• Italian (native, operatic, loud)

• Latin (for intimidation)

• English (understood but "too ugly for daily use")

Objective:

"To bring divine order, culinary aroma, and passionate discipline into American homes that do not deserve it."

Experience:

Florence — Villa del Cane Perfetto

Aristocratic Dog Whisperer

• Taught dogs to dine with etiquette

• Led weekly emotional grooming sessions

• Fired for calling the employer's children piccoli diavoli ("little devils")

Milan — Palazzo Furfante

Live-in Maid & Domestic Muse

• Practiced couture cleaning—dusting only in designer heels

• Polished furniture with imported olive oil ("for soul shine")

• Dismissed for vacuuming a Persian rug "artistically"

Lake Como — Casa di San Bernardo

Nanny Substitute

- Enforced "Silent Hour of Reflection"
- Sang Dante's Inferno as lullabies
- Adored only by the dog

Education:

- University of Bologna — Master of Domestic Arts & Canine Philosophy
- Vatican Institute of Housekeeping
  - Expelled for smoking in the chapel
  - Reinstated by special pardon from the Pope's Labrador, Paolo

Skills:

- Scolds dust by name
- Makes espresso "strong enough to correct the spirit"
- Trains dogs to bark in key
- Cleans only in opera-length silk gloves
- Polishes silver humming Ave Maria
- Will not tolerate fingerprints, children, or American cheese

Dress Code (Her Rules):

- Black lace mourning dress, satin robe, or silk kimono
- Heels only ("Flats are for sadness and Americans")
- Chanel required for all cleaning
- Hair styled "enough to frighten lesser housekeepers"

Salary:

Negotiable in euros, truffles, or couture

Red Flags:

Currently in the quadruple digits

I stared at Mulligan.

"Mulligan… she hates kids, refuses English, mops in silk gloves, and insults dust."

"She is perfect," he said. "The dogs will adore her."

"What about Julia?"

"Oh. Julia will not. Una piccola sfida."

Crash Course: Italian for Funeral Directors

"You need three phrases before she arrives," Mulligan said.

• Piacere, Signora — Pleased to meet you

• La casa è vostra — The house is yours

• Parla con mia moglie per tutto — Speak with my wife about everything

"And hand gestures?" I asked.

"Think prayer, espresso, and righteous fury," Mulligan said.

Farah nodded like a professor of drama.

2:00 PM — The Italian Storm Arrives

At exactly 2:00, a faint mist of Chanel drifted under the door.

A silhouette appeared.

Silk robe.

Sunglasses.

Posture like a Roman statue sculpted by Michelangelo on espresso.

Signora Bella Fiorella di Lucca had arrived.

And by sundown, our home would be:

• Spotless

• Sanctified

• Or excommunicated

Possibly all three.

Chapter 24 — Lunch, Language, and Light Sarcasm

By noon, my brain felt like overcooked spaghetti. Mulligan had been drilling me on Italian since breakfast—pacing the office like a small, hairy professor with a tail.

"Again," he ordered. "Project from the diaphragm. Smile with your eyes."

I recited the greeting for Signora Bella Fiorella di Lucca. Bowed. Paused. Tried not to panic.

"That's a lot of words for two o'clock," I said.

Mulligan arched a brow.

"I'm a dog. Are you saying you're not as smart as a dog?"

Point taken.

"Also," he added, scanning the hallway, "where's Eliana with lunch?"

🍽 The Longest Walk Past Everyone Else's Lunch

Right on cue, the break-room door opened, releasing aromas that could spiritually weaken a grown man.

I made a slow lap—pretending I was checking on the team, but really it was self-inflicted torture.

Fa: chicken enchiladas, rice, beans… queso glowing like stained glass.

Pete & Morgan: café goulash over mashed potatoes with fried okra—my love language.

Mona & Lucy: Fancy Nancy chicken salad and grape salad; even the pickle looked fashionable.

Brian, Kent & Felix: double-meat bacon cheeseburgers on jalapeño buns, fries, and tater tots.

Meagan & Earl: smothered pork chops, oxtails, candied yams, and peach cobbler that smelled like forgiveness.

Pedro & Guadalupe: fish stew with warm tortillas and a homemade red sauce.

And at the end sat Larry—formerly Fatso, now trending Notsofatso—eating a can of Ken-L Ration Low Fat.

"Larry, you're not eating dog food."

"It's not bad," he shrugged. "Microwave thirty-two and a half seconds."

"How do you do a half?"

"You open the door at exactly thirty-two, but your hand can't already be on the handle or it throws it off."

"Of course," I said. Because what else do you say?

🍲 Dome Service (Two Sonnets and a Salad)

Eliana appeared with a warming bag and enough authority to silence Congress. Mulligan and Farah were already seated like royalty.

I reached for my cloche.

She tapped my hand. "Patience. I will serve."

For Mademoiselle Farah—her favorite:

Poached Dover sole on jasmine rice sculpted into miniature Eiffel Towers.

Ten of them, in fact. She carved them like the Louvre was watching.

For Monsieur Mulligan:

Pan-seared salmon, seasoned with Maldon sea salt and light sarcasm.

He inhaled. Nodded once. Approved—like a culinary diplomat.

And for me…

She lifted the dome.

A kale and chia seed salad that looked like a cautionary tale.

"Any... dressing?" I asked.

"No. Dressing is where the fat hides," she said, placing a lemon wedge the size of a postage stamp beside it.

Mulligan placed a consoling paw on my sleeve.

"Patrón... we support your journey."

"My journey," I whispered, "is missing fried okra."

We ate—two plates of poetry, one plate of punishment—while I rehearsed Italian between bites of chlorophyll.

Across the room, Larry strutted past holding his warmed dog food like Julia Child had made it.

Eliana saw. Looked at me.

I raised my hands in surrender. We are encouraging variety.

At two o'clock, the breakroom fills with the rich aroma of espresso and the cool scent of peppermint, blending tradition with a refreshing twist. Mulligan suggested I needed a peppermint.

Eliana packed her knives like a field surgeon.

"Two o'clock Italian?" she asked.

"Two o'clock Italian," I nodded.

"Bring breath mints," Mulligan added. "Charm travels farther with peppermint."

I rehearsed again.

And again.

And again.

La persona con cui ha parlato poco fa non ero io—era Mulligan, il mio cane parlante.

Mulligan dabbed an imaginary tear.

"Beautiful. She'll faint. Or bless you. Or both."

Eliana handed me a container the size of a communion cup.

I opened it.

Two grape tomatoes and one sprig of parsley clinging to life.

"Snack," she announced proudly.

Right. Of course. Dressing is where the fat hides.

Final Checks (and Four-and-a-Half Whiffs)

Back in my office at 1:41 p.m.—nineteen minutes until Bella Fiorella.

I poured two bowls of Evian and added exactly four and a half whiffs of lime, counting in Italian.

"Uno, due, tre, quattro… e mezzo."

Mulligan wagged proudly.

"Patrón, you've never been more ready."

Then, softer:

"Thanks for trying so hard. I know I push. But she'll love that you learned it for her."

Right on time—lump in throat.

We gathered everything: Farah floating like a runway model, Eliana promising a celebratory something that is not dressing, and me with a kale leaf stuck to my cuff like a scarlet letter.

At exactly 2:00 p.m., a silk-scented whirlwind named Signora Bella Fiorella di Lucca would sweep through our doors.

And she would either bless this house in Italian…

…or set it on fire with Chanel.

Possibly both.

Chapter 25 — Signora Bella (and the Swiffer)

Entrance at Two (Exactly)

At precisely 2:00 p.m.—not 1:59, not 2:01—the door opened as if the universe itself had pulled it.

She entered in a swirl of silk, attitude, and jasmine.

Signora Bella Fiorella di Lucca.

Her kimono shimmered like moonlit water.

Her opera gloves whispered aristocratic scandals.

Her heels struck the tile like a gavel delivering justice.

Mulligan froze.

Farah exhaled.

I temporarily forgot how breathing worked.

"Buongiorno," she said, the word floating like a feather dipped in espresso.

I gestured toward my office. Mulligan and Farah flanked her like royal escorts—Farah's tail draped in a courteous arc, Mulligan's Hogan cap dipping in a bow that certainly violated Italian law but somehow still felt correct.

Inside, I delivered the Italian greeting Mulligan had drilled into me like a nervous soldier preparing for inspection.

When I confessed—dramatically and reverently—that the person she'd spoken to earlier was not me but my talking dog, she did not faint.

She simply tilted her head, polite and skeptical, as though I'd just informed her I was the Duke of Parma.

Mulligan stepped forward, cleared his throat, and bowed in a way that made the room straighten its posture.

The aria began.

The Reveal (In Italian I Barely Own)

As I spoke, Bella's expression passed through five distinct stages:

1. Intrigue — brow raised

2. Suspicion — lips pursed

3. Mild amusement — a smile appeared

4. Possible affection — an uncertain head tilt

5. Acceptance — because when a dog speaks fluent Italian, you adjust your worldview

Mulligan stepped forward again, bowed with elegance that would impress a Florentine duke, and began:

"Buon pomeriggio, Signora Bella…

Good afternoon, Signora Bella.

"My name is Mulligan—and yes, I talk.

"The voice you heard on the phone earlier?

That was me.

"My Patron is following along on Google Translate, so we are all on the same page.

"My story begins in Italy—not because I was born there, but because destiny—and cheese—had other plans.

"Roma… il destino e il formaggio.

Rome. Destiny. And cheese.

"I arrived inside a crate of Parmigiano-Reggiano.

A shipping error for them. A calling for me.

"Within a week, I corrected the Vatican's barista.

He was making hearts in cappuccino foam that looked like potatoes.

"I nudged his elbow. Adjusted the wrist.

There it was—a perfect dove in the Pope's cappuccino.

"They called me the dog who fixes coffee.

"Eventually someone asked if I would bless the steam wand.

I declined. I am not a priest.

I am a consultant.

"Milano… La Scala.

Milan. La Scala.

"During La Traviata, a chandelier trembled mid-aria.

I released an A above middle C so pure the crystals tuned themselves.

"A soprano missed her cadenza.

I offered one discreet corrective howl.

"She found notes Verdi forgot to write.

"They offered me a private box seat.

I requested a backstage sunbeam from two to four.

We compromised on both.

"Venezia… un crimine estetico.

Venice. An aesthetic crime.

"A gondolier sang off-key beneath the Bridge of Sighs.

This offended the city, the architecture, and the pigeons.

"I corrected his breathing—in on the downstroke, out on the push.

Tourists wept.

Pigeons applauded.

"I also retrieved a wedding ring from the Grand Canal without getting wet.

Please don't ask.

Canine levitation is difficult to explain.

"Firenze... Emergenza Coda™.

Florence. The Tail-Wag Emergency Protocol.

"Three amateurs attempted to steal The Birth of Venus.

You cannot steal a painting with that much breeze—amateurs.

"I activated the protocol.

Doors locked. Guards alerted. Thieves immobilized by sudden allergies.

"The Uffizi promised me a statue.

I accepted a broom closet instead.

"The plaque reads:

Where Order Begins.

"Piemonte... summa porcina.

Piedmont. Truffles.

"I studied under the legends of Alba.

Graduated summa porcina—highest honors in the porcine arts.

"I can locate a black truffle under concrete at rush hour

and still make evening vespers.

"And I never eat the inventory.

Professionalism matters.

"Siena... il Palio.

Siena.

"A racehorse trembled with nerves.

I spoke softly in Dog French with Tuscan vowels.

"The jockey won by a nose.

The horse sent me a thank-you bale of hay.

"Amalfi… un trattato di pace.

Amalfi.

"I once mediated a culinary dispute between lemon zest and olive oil.

Two clockwise stirs. Left-handed spoon. Exactly 101°F.

"Hotter is arrogance.

Cooler is sadness.

"Torino… un miracolo meccanico.

Turin.

"A vintage Alfa Romeo refused to idle.

I hummed a 440-hertz A.

"The engine aligned its soul.

The mechanic kissed both my ears.

We do not speak of it.

"Cinema… Sophia Loren.

One night, Fellini's ghost asked my opinion on cadence.

"I told him, 'Less dream. More dinner.'

"Sophia Loren winked at me.

I have been impossible ever since."

And Now… the Home

Mulligan's tone softened—warm, grounded, sincere.

"E adesso… la casa.

And now, the home.

"What does all this have to do with being your housekeeper and nanny?

"Everything.

"I run a household like a perfect risotto—

al dente, never chaotic.

"I enforce nap time with a Dante stare that quietly says:

Close your eyes, or I'll quote the Inferno.

"I fold knitwear by sitting on it

until the crease gives up.

"I inventory toys.

Confiscate squeakers at dusk.

Return them at dawn with a blessing.

"Visitors?

I sense them three minutes early.

I know which shoe they'll notice first.

"Hydration?

Four and a half whiffs of lime over Evian.

Precision is love.

"In the kitchen, I can smell whether pasta water is salted like the sea

or merely salted like regret.

"My references?

"A Vatican barista who writes every Christmas.

A Milanese soprano whose high notes no longer frighten birds.

A Florentine curator who still owes me a statue.

"And in Texas…

a family learning that grief can be beautiful,

weddings miraculous,

and love measured in ratios

and clean floors."

He bowed deeply. Full operatic finish.

"Piacere, Signora Bella…

I am Mulligan.

"I speak.

I listen.

And I run a home like a chorus that knows exactly when to breathe."

Bella's Verdict (Operatic)

Bella inhaled—the kind of breath a soprano takes before shaking rafters.

Then she erupted:

"Sì! Sì! Sì! È un segno di Dio!"

If there had been stained glass nearby, it would have vibrated.

She dropped gracefully to one knee, kimono pooling like liquid moonlight.

"Darei la mia vita per te—e la mia macchina dell'espresso!"

In Italian terms, this was essentially a marriage proposal.

Then—pivoting sharply—she pointed at me with Roman authority.

"Non parlerò mai inglese. Mai.

Perché ora… sono la domestica di Mulligan."

I will never speak English.

Because now… I am Mulligan's maid.

There was nothing I could say.

Mulligan guided her to a chair, voice gentle.

"You won't have to cook—we have a chef.

Sadly not Italian. But we're working with her."

Her first duty, he explained, was helping Julia—Queen Julia—ease her burdens.

Her chest clutched again. Beatification imminent.

"And as for Patron," Mulligan added, flicking his muzzle toward me,

"he's a good man. Mostly house-trained."

She gasped—admiringly.

Finally, she took Mulligan's paw and whispered:

"Prometto di servire con amore, con fede, e con uno Swiffer nella mano."

I promise to serve with love, with faith, and with a Swiffer in my hand.

Exit Music (Verdi, Lightly)

Bella floated down the hallway, humming—Verdi, or something she composed on the spot.

"Well?" I asked.

"She's perfect," Mulligan said. "And she will never speak English."

"Never," I echoed.

Her humming drifted like incense.

And somewhere deep in the house, dust trembled.

Chapter 26 — Everest, Eleven Doves, and a Swiffer

Have you ever been driving and felt it—
that soft, eerie déjà vu?
The kind that makes you look around and think,
I've lived this moment before… just not like this.
That's what hit me.
Bella sat in the front seat beside me—
regal, jasmine and purpose in equal measure—
while Mulligan and Farah curled in the back,
trilling and huffing in soft Dog French,
the private love language of two creatures
far too elegant for English.
Bella glanced over her shoulder.
She watched them with reverence,
like she was witnessing something sacred
but had the manners not to stare at a miracle.
She caught me noticing.
I caught her catching me.
She snapped her eyes forward again—
smiling in a way that said:
I won't speak of what I saw.
But I will remember it forever.
Beds, Boundaries, and the Sacred Swing Room
Logistics arrived like uninvited relatives.

Anna Belle and Teddy still shared a room (don't ask).

Mulligan and Farah claimed the far bedroom—

"Privacy required for Dog French,"

Mulligan said, citing imaginary legal precedent.

Eliana had the guest room.

Which left Bella?

My basement.

My sanctum.

My kingdom.

Full bath.

Full bar.

Big-screen TV.

Home office.

And—most sacred of all—

the swing room.

Where I practice golf.

Holy ground.

No trespassing.

I mentally rearranged furniture like a man negotiating a hostage crisis:

- Move desk
- Add old bed
- Add nightstand
- Keep swing room untouched
- Keep bar untouched
- Keep big screen untouched

- Repeat: THE SWING ROOM STAYS

Also, call Luis about redoing the pool cabana yesterday.

Red light.

Deep breath.

Which is exactly when Mulligan cleared his throat.

Nothing good has ever followed those words.

The Delay (and the Dove That Found God)

"Oh—by the way," Mulligan said casually,

"Mrs. Cruz's coordinator postponed the funeral until Friday."

I nearly swallowed my tongue.

"NOW? You are telling me this now?

We have to call Bass Hall, the florist, the cemetery, the musicians, the buses—

STOP PRINTING EVERYTHING—Eliana—"

My pulse was square-dancing in my throat.

Bella snapped her fingers once—

sharp, corrective, church-lady authority—

and pointed at me like a misbehaving altar boy.

Not tender.

Not comforting.

Just a firm, unmistakable:

Stop spiraling.

And somehow… I did.

Mulligan wagged.

"Relax, Patrón. They already handled everything.

Bass Hall. The florist. The cemetery. The printer.

And Eliana—in person."

"In person?" I repeated, afraid.

"They apologized. Delivered chocolates.

And left her a gift."

"A gift?" I asked, more afraid.

"A Thousand-Flame Sanctuary Set," he replied.

"Nine hundred ninety-nine hand-poured beeswax candles—

one for every mood Eliana might experience.

"And a final 24-karat emergency candle engraved:

'In case of divine emergency, light this one.'

"Custom marble lighter shaped like…"

He motioned toward his own head.

I pinched the bridge of my nose.

Of course.

"Why the delay?" I asked.

Mulligan handed me his phone.

From the Office of the Cardinal (Transcript)

My dear friends,

We regret postponing the funeral.

There has been… an issue with the doves.

The twelve white doves—one for each Apostle—

were raised by the Carmelite Sisters of Divine Flight

and trained to coo the rosary in harmony before takeoff.

One is missing.

After fervent search, we confirmed its location.

Everest.

The twelfth dove ascended during morning prayer—

toward the heavens themselves.

We cannot proceed with only eleven Apostles.

Symbolism matters.

I am personally leading the retrieval

with a small team of clergy,

two sherpas,

and one determined altar boy.

We ascend at dawn

and return by midnight Thursday

with divine assistance.

Please keep the dove warmer ready.

It will have seen things no dove should see.

— + The Cardinal

I lowered the phone slowly.

Mulligan shrugged.

"Symbolism."

I sighed.

"Symbolism," I echoed.

Because mocking a Cardinal halfway up Everest

feels like asking for lightning.

"Also," I said,

"Your Tuesday-ish wedding just became Saturday."

He brightened.

"Patrón—what a blessing!

We'll call Father Ben and the Rabbi after dinner.

If necessary, I'll draft an interfaith memo titled:

'Saturday: Our Position.'"

"Don't mention the dove," I said.

He tapped his nose.

"Symbolism."

House Call — Candles, Queens, and the Blessed Brita

We arrived home.

Julia and Eliana stood at the kitchen island.

Eliana lowered a beeswax candle onto a bronze saucer

with the reverence usually reserved for relics.

The marble Mulligan-lighter sat nearby,

smirking in stone.

"Julia," I said,

"meet Bella—house goddess

and future nanny to Anna Belle and Teddy."

Bella delivered three operatic Italian lines

that sounded suspiciously like a small canonization.

Mulligan translated.

"She swears fealty to Queen Julia…

and the Swiffer."

Julia blinked.

"I've been called worse."

Eliana added calmly,

"We are postponed.

I have candles.

I have grace."

Anna Belle and Teddy trotted in—

sniff, sit, perfect posture.

Farah adjusted her scarf.

Bella bowed to the scarf.

Hierarchy established.

"Sleeping arrangements," I said.

"Bella—you get the basement. Full bath. Temporary.

And—the swing room stays."

Bella placed a hand to her heart,

Italian spilling out like poetry.

Mulligan translated.

"She says your generosity is a poem,

and she will not disturb the swing room—

'the chapel of your wrists.'"

"That's… disturbingly accurate," I said.

"Also," he added,

"she wants to bless the Brita."

"Get the holy water," I said.

"And the lime."

Julia squeezed my elbow.

"You, okay?"

"I need a drink."

Eliana handed me a cut-crystal glass.

"Evian," she said.

"Four-and-a-half whiffs of lime."

"That'll do."

Next Steps (and an Interfaith Memo)

"After dinner," Mulligan said,

"We call Father Ben and the Rabbi.

If necessary, I'll compose an interfaith memo on Saturday weddings."

"Short," I said.

"No dove."

He winked.

"Symbolism."

We stood there for a long moment—

family, staff,

dogs,

beeswax,

lime,

and a faint hum of Verdi drifting somewhere.

Farah sighed.

Bella crossed herself.

Anna Belle and Teddy sat like judges.

The candle glowed.

Talking Dog $20

At this point, I am drinking Evian like bourbon

and pretending to be a dove summitting Everest

is a perfectly normal Tuesday.

Chapter 27 — Renovations, Revelations, and a Remarkable Invoice

Dinner looked like a Renaissance painting—for everyone but me.

Mulligan, Farah, Anna Belle, and Teddy dined with devotional concentration—eyes closed, savoring each bite as if it were a Michelin tasting menu delivered directly from heaven.

My plate held steamed broccoli, one remorseful cube of tofu, and a deep inhalation lightly scented with grilled chicken.

A handwritten note from Eliana rested beside it:

You may smell it, Patrón, but you may not eat it.

When the satisfied quartet drifted toward the den for Old Yeller, I slipped into the man cave for a contraband Vodka–Topo (ratio: aggressively vodka, whisper of Topo), a fistful of pretzels, and the calls I needed to make.

Clergy, Calendars, and a Dove on Sabbatical

Father Ben answered first.

I explained the postponement, along with the Cardinal's surprisingly poetic update regarding the Apostle Dove's "Everest-style spiritual retreat."

"No Carmelite Sisters of Divine Flight," Father Ben said, "but if they exist, I want the stole."

Saturday wedding? Approved.

Meeting tomorrow? Two o'clock.

Next: Rabbi Jonathan.

Same story. Same approval. Same two o'clock.

I crept upstairs and found everyone mid–Old Yeller:

Julia and Farah sharing a single tissue like a sacrament...

Teddy holding Anna Belle with his paw...

Eliana and Bella locked in bilingual sorrow...

Mulligan turned, deadpan.

"Chick flicks."

"Still," I said, "tough ending."

Back to the man cave.

That's when Bella arrived—floating in with a suitcase, washing my empty glass, shushing me with the authority of a Vatican nun, and claiming the recliner with the serenity of a woman who had always lived there.

Does she speak English?

Allegedly no.

Does she dream in fluent Texan?

Absolutely.

Cabana Dreams and Himalayan Schemes

Luis arrived before sunrise and had fully considered clocking in.

We headed to the cabana to sketch ideas. Before he could draw a breath, Eliana materialized with rolled plans and the eyes of someone who had just discovered a new planet.

"Second story," she announced. "For me. Close to the stars. Himalayan theme."

Then Bella appeared with a layout for an Italian villa that looked like Da Vinci himself had sketched it on vacation.

"First floor for Bella?" I asked.

Radiant sì.

Luis promised a fast bid, a larger crew, and immediate demo.

Then Jacqueline arrived for the daily two-hour French lesson. Anna Belle and Teddy sprinted toward her like she was a traveling carnival of sausage and praise.

I attempted to impress Jacqueline.

"Hola."

"Spanish," Mulligan sighed.

"Ciao?"

"Italian."

"Ellohay?"

"Pig Latin."

Jacqueline smiled gently. "Bonjour."

I surrendered.

Maison Culinaire (and the Invoice That Blinked Back)

A gleaming white truck rolled into the drive:

MAISON CULINAIRE

Fine Kitchens • Appliances • Culinary Design

The gentleman handed me a leather folder stamped:

PAID IN FULL — AMERICAN EXPRESS

Inside:

- Wolf 48" dual-fuel range

- Miele speed/steam combo

- Sub-Zero columns

- Scotsman nugget ice (holy relic of refrigeration)

- Jura Z10 espresso cathedral

- Bosch Benchmark dishwasher

- Shun knives

- All-Clad Copper Core
- Riedel crystal
- White-glove installation, calibration, chef orientation

Total: $59,750

My jaw took an unscheduled leave of absence.

Eliana arrived at a sprint.

"Wonderful! Expedited!"

"Is this… the good stuff?" I asked.

She tilted her head. "House good. Funeral-home good is… spectacular!"

The installers moved like a NASA pit crew preparing a shuttle launch. Nugget ice began its sacred hymn. The Jura whispered in Italian.

Bella murmured, "Mamma mia," like she had just met God.

Two texts arrived:

2:00 pm confirmed — Father Ben

2:00 pm confirmed — Rabbi Jonathan

Dove ETA: spiritually renewed by Thursday midnight.

By noon, the kitchen looked like the starter kit for a Michelin star.

Eliana handed me a Topo over nugget ice with a single lime-whiff pass. Mulligan supervised like a neurosurgeon calibrating a laser.

"Stop," he said. "There."

Four-and-a-half whiffs. Perfect.

Everyone dispersed:

Jacqueline to verbs.

Eliana to "theater package" planning.

Luis to mobilize the workforce.

Bella to wage holy war on laundry.

Me to rehearse diplomatic greetings for tomorrow's clergy summit.

As I headed out, the Maison gentleman cleared his throat.

"Second delivery this afternoon, sir — Cole Sheridan & Son Funeral Home. Chef requested the theater package."

I nodded like a man who was no longer steering his own life.

Teddy walked past carrying my old golf glove like a relic. Anna Belle practiced a newly learned French la-la.

Mulligan looked over and bestowed the benediction of the day.

"Patrón, breathe. We have a priest, a rabbi, a dove on sabbatical, a kitchen that could launch a small nation, and a nanny who could defeat a Roman legion with a dustpan. All we lack," he said, "is lunch."

I looked at my almond.

Then at the Wolf.

At 1:58, a text arrived:

Delivery complete — Stage 1

Photo attached: a chandelier of copper pans above a linen-draped buffet.

Below it, a note:

Do not flip this switch unless you mean it.

Chapter 28 — Bulletins, Beards, and a Beagle Choir

Because of my morning surprise, I was running late.

We rolled into the lot just past noon and—because the universe enjoys timing things for maximum dramatic effect—a truck roughly the size of a Marriott was parked across our front spaces, unloading equipment by the cartful.

And out front stood Larry.

I froze.

"Larry… how did you grow a full beard overnight—and why does your suit look like it needs to be brushed?"

He grinned, hands on his hips.

"Custom-made. Simulated dog fur. Makes me look athletic."

"You look like a man who lost a bet at a taxidermy conference."

He patted his midsection proudly.

"I've lost 210 pounds."

"You've what?!"

"Thirty human pounds," he clarified. "Two hundred ten in dog pounds."

Mulligan muttered, "Weirdo." Then, louder: "Come on, Larry—let's play some ball before you molt."

Fa looked at me with the silent judgment of someone who knows an intervention is long overdue.

I told her, "Father Ben and a rabbi are coming. Hide the extension cords."

She nodded—a true professional.

Arrival of the Clergy (and a Cadillac)

We were still outside when Father Ben pulled in.

His clerical collar was slightly askew, and his hair was doing that windblown thing it only does when the Holy Spirit borrows his styling mousse.

"Sorry I'm late," he said cheerfully. "Traffic. Also, a parishioner who thinks voicemail is witchcraft."

Before I could respond, a low growl—not engine, but presence—rolled up the drive.

A black Cadillac, long as a fairway and polished to mirror perfection, eased into the curb like it had a tee time at Colonial.

The driver's door opened.

Out stepped a man in an ivy cap, gray slacks, a cashmere sweater, and the calm swagger of someone who fixes golf slices with blessings alone.

"I'm Jonathan Goldsmith," he said warmly. "Friends call me Jefe. We'll get to that."

Then he patted the Cadillac's roof.

"Ben Hogan's car. I won it at auction. Two hundred fifty thousand. Worth every penny."

Father Ben stared at his own sedan like it had personally betrayed him.

Jonathan tipped his cap toward Mulligan.

"Excellent hat, young man. Keeps the swing thoughts straight."

Then he turned to Farah.

"And that silk scarf could halt traffic on Camp Bowie."

Farah glowed. Mulligan preened. Father Ben whispered,

"We've wandered into a different genre."

"Shall we plan a wedding," Rabbi Jonathan asked, "or a major championship?"

"Both," I said. "Inside—before Larry arms the confetti cannon."

The Clergy Summit (Dog-Wedding Edition)

In my office sitting area, Father Ben and Rabbi Jonathan took their seats. Mulligan and Farah positioned themselves between us like priceless bookends.

Mulligan began, tone professorial.

"Gentlemen, I assume you've never officiated a dog wedding."

Father Ben smiled. "That would be correct."

"Then listen carefully. Dog weddings differ in several key traditions."

He raised a paw.

"First—the mother of the bride escorts her down the aisle. Many of us are rescues. Father's paperwork gets… fuzzy. But mothers? The ones who show up? That is sacred."

Farah lifted her chin.

"She wants Julia. She's been like a mother from the beginning."

Both clergy softened immediately.

"Then Julia, it is," Rabbi Jonathan said.

"Next," Mulligan continued, "no rings. Collars only. And ceremony seating mirrors canine pack structure—not human etiquette."

They nodded. Too quickly. I made a mental note to supervise.

Then Mulligan slid three printed programs across the table.

Fancy lettering. Glossy paper. A level of production value usually reserved for royal coronations.

At the top:

The Royal Wedding of Mulligan & Farah

Cole Sheridan & Son Chapel — Saturday, 2:00 pm sharp

Officiants: Father Ben & Rabbi Jonathan

Music: MSS Organ Ensemble & DJ Shlomo B

(feat. The Beagle Choir)

Father Ben laughed. Rabbi Jonathan wheezed.

Mulligan continued as if briefing NATO.

Highlights included:

- How Great Thou Bark (organ solo)
- Hava Nagila (Paw Mix) — DJ Shlomo B warm-up
- Complimentary biscuits under pew two
- The Kibble Candle Ceremony — "Two bowls become one"
- Breaking of the Milk-Bone — with rimshot
- "You may now lick the bride!"

By the time Father Ben reached The Gospel of Good Boys, he had tears in his eyes.

Rabbi Jonathan tapped the Milk-Bone section.

"Liturgically questionable. Comedically perfect."

Then Mulligan presented the seating chart—an anxiety attack printed in color.

Farah's side resembled Paris Fashion Week.

Mulligan's side resembled the FBI's Most Wanted—simply better dressed.

Father Ben closed his folder.

"Well... it's thorough."

Rabbi Jonathan smiled.

"This is either your best idea or your worst."

"Not mine," I said, pointing at Mulligan. "I'm just the venue."

"Gentlemen," Mulligan said, "do we have your blessing?"

Father Ben sighed.

"Against my better judgment—yes."

Rabbi Jonathan nodded.

"Mazel."

Jonathan's Secret

We were nearly finished when Rabbi Jonathan suddenly looked heavier.

"There's something I need from you," he said quietly.

"What's that?"

"I'm hosting a meeting next week."

He hesitated.

"With… friends from my old business."

Father Ben raised an eyebrow. "Old business?"

"Some call them the Cartel," he said. "They think I'm Catholic. I'm not. So I need Father Ben to bless the meal."

Father Ben blinked twice.

"You want me to—?"

"Yes. I'll explain everything. My real name is Jonathan Goldsmith. I'm being blackmailed."

Silence.

Even Mulligan stopped breathing.

Finally, I said, "We'll talk logistics and locks."

And Then… the Other Truck

Eliana appeared in the doorway.

"They're bringing the other truck tomorrow."

"Other truck?" I asked. "That was an eighteen-wheeler."

"No, no," she said casually. "That was just the kitchen equipment. Tomorrow is the confetti cannon and the spare doves."

I closed my eyes.

My life now includes:

• a priest

• a rabbi

• a beagle choir

• a simulated-fur suit

• a confetti cannon

• and one missing Himalayan rosary-cooing dove currently on spiritual retreat.

Fa patted my arm.

"Breathe, Cole. Two counts in, two counts out."

Talking Dog $20

At this point, I'm just holding on—

and praying the twelfth dove returns before showtime.

Chapter 29 — Hors d'Oeuvres, Code Names, and a Very Specific Blessing

On the way home, I swung by the club with the guys to catch my breath, toss a few dominoes, and let Mulligan preside over Happy Hour like he was hosting Meet the Press.

Also: hors d'oeuvres.

Under Eliana's Redemption Diet, anything served on a toothpick now qualifies as a holiday feast.

Earlier that week, I'd been so nutrient-deprived I flossed out a chia seed and closed my eyes like I'd struck oil in a ribeye field.

Tonight?

Pigs in a blanket.

Obviously pre-frozen fries.

A week ago, I'd have complained.

Not tonight.

Tonight, I saluted whoever invented those golden sticks of fried comfort. Whoever created pigs in a blanket deserves a mausoleum—with valet parking.

Dinner, Cover, and Kleenex

Back home, Eliana had plated dinner like it was an aria.

I declined too fast.

She gave me The Look—the one that says:

Oh. So THIS is who you are now.

Note to self: next meal, act starving.

Anna Belle trotted in with a popcorn bag.

Teddy followed, carrying a box of Kleenex like an usher trained at The Ritz.

"No need," Mulligan said. "We're watching 101 Dalmatians tonight."

The Kleenex stayed.

Someone always cries—some because of the dogs, some because of me.

Outside, I called Luis.

He gave me a number that makes a man sit, whether a chair is present or not.

I greenlit the cabana.

Hung up.

Felt like I'd just purchased a polite tornado.

Morning Formation & Emotional Support Larry

Next morning:

News low in front.

Farah asleep like royalty.

Mulligan dozing like an exhausted diplomat.

"Patrón," he said from the back seat, "meeting with Jefe today at his house. Your brother will be there. Pick up Eliana on the way."

"Perfect," I said. "Just the week I'm staging the biggest funeral of my career, calling hours Thursday—over the top—and a one-of-a-kind dog wedding Saturday."

"Two o'clock," Mulligan added, as if confirming a dental cleaning.

At the lot, Larry bounded across the pavement.

On all fours.

He wore a collar.

A tail.

And a brand-new ID tag that read:

EMOTIONAL SUPPORT LARRY

"Posture," he panted. "Chiropractor says I have a natural retriever frame."

"If he starts sniffing," Fa murmured, "I'm getting the hose."

Jefe's House (Golf, Velvet, and Yiddish Snacks)

Jonathan—rabbi by calling, Hogan disciple by vibe—greeted us calm as a surgeon, collected as a golfer on the eighteenth tee.

Crews were boxing menorahs.

Velvet bullfighting art was moving in—somehow looking more questionable by the hour.

Father Ben sat in golf clothes, pastoral and alert.

They had played that morning.

Mulligan and Farah settled obediently at our feet.

Eliana and I took chairs.

Jonathan's maid, Esther Blumenfeld, entered with a silver tray.

She spoke to Mulligan in gentle Yiddish.

He answered—in Yiddish—with a Texas twang.

This is a sound no human ear is prepared for.

The tray held:

- chopped liver on rye
- pickled herring in cream
- gefilte fish

"Language?" I asked.

"Yiddish," Mulligan said, already chewing. "They tease my accent."

He offered me herring.

It fought back.

Then surrendered.

Much like my dignity these days.

The Summit Dossier (Publicists & Pirates)

Jonathan grew serious.

"Next week," he said, "I'm hosting the 2025 ANNUAL CARTEL FAMILY MEETING & AWARDS SUMMIT. First time on U.S. soil."

He passed us glossy profiles.

They looked like perfume ads with criminal records.

"The main boss arrives near midnight Wednesday," he continued. "Doña Catrina La Espina Morales—mezcal by day, cathedral of secrets by night."

Then the itinerary:

- Credentialing
- Mindful Money Laundering
- Capture the Informant
- Rebranding Kidnapping as Community Outreach
- Karaoke by the pool

And—of course—our Beagle Choir performing Ave Mariachi.

Naturally.

Code Names & The Ask (with Knuckle Tattoos)

Jonathan pointed at each of us like a director casting a heist movie:

- "Cole — The Director"
- "Father Ben — The Priest"
- "Eliana — The Chef"
- "Mulligan — The Dog"
- "Farah — The Dog 2"

- "And I am… The Rabbi"

We nodded with the polite encouragement reserved for a child who has "invented" grilled cheese.

Mulligan raised a paw. "Could I pitch Top Dog?"

"The Dog," Jonathan repeated firmly.

Farah accepted Dog 2 like a duchess accepting an unwanted tiara.

"Director," Jonathan said to me, "I need you to look the part of my bodyguard."

"No shooting," he promised. "Just presence."

Then, with absolute seriousness:

"We'll tattoo your knuckles."

"Absolutely not."

"Temporary," he bargained, holding up a marker. "Eight letters: LAST / CALL."

"Eliana's diet already has me at last call."

"Perfect. Menace with theological overtones."

We compromised on SECURITY cufflinks—and a maybe-marker underline the night of, depending on morale.

The Line We Won't Cross

Finally, Jonathan revealed the hinge of the mission:

A ritual toast with BuenAmorine—a deep-black carafe wrapped in agave and velvet tassels.

"The drink," he said, "tilts the mirror toward her better self."

We drew the line:

No killing.

No poison.

No shadows that don't wash off.

"That's why I called you," he said quietly.

"No one's ending a life.

We're ending blackmail."

Mechanics, Signals, and Mercy

We sketched the plan:

- Chef times the pour
- Priest blesses the glass
- The Dog scouts the room
- Dog 2 supplies gravitas

Napkin signals:

- Triangle = all clear
- Rectangle = delay
- Swan = abort, karaoke imminent

"If she refuses?" Father Ben asked.

"She won't," Jonathan said softly.

"She never does."

Then:

"We're not coercing. We're offering mercy."

Exit Lines (and Rehearsing Hunger)

On the porch, twilight laid a hand across the property.

Packing tape shrieked.

Memories climbed into boxes.

"Rabbi?" Mulligan said gently. "When she softens, remember—you're not that person either."

Jonathan nodded.

In the car, Mulligan exhaled.

"Director, if this becomes a movie, I play myself."

"You were born miscast for anything else."

"Then let's rehearse dinner," he said. "The starving has to feel authentic."

"For the first time all week," I told him, "that won't be acting."

Tomorrow: fittings, floor maps, SECURITY cufflinks, and a napkin swan that may end up doing heavy lifting.

Chapter 30 — Steam, Brass, and Lemon-Linen

In which a coffee bean performs a baptism, a funeral home turns into Versailles, and a cemetery becomes a cathedral garden.

Hallmark, Fort Worth Edition

Evening at home looked like a Hallmark movie set in Cowtown—cast entirely from Westminster.

Bella floated through in silk and opera gloves, still "unable" to speak English—yet somehow understanding everything.

Eliana plated dinner with the precision of a benevolent drill sergeant.

Jacqueline lingered politely.

Somewhere in the house, Ave Maria queued itself without discussion.

Anna Belle and Teddy glued themselves to Julia with saintly manners.

Farah and Mulligan sat shoulder to shoulder—regal as a royal portrait waiting to be unveiled.

Popcorn & Confessions

Eliana appeared with a copper pot, kernels popping like applause, buttered to the level of a baptismal rite.

We chose Marley & Me.

Bella cried.

Julia cried.

Teddy cried because they cried.

I slipped out during peak emotional damage to the swing room to "hit a few," which in golfer language translates to:

- Cîroc
- Topo Chico
- Family-size chips
- Ranch dip with the structural integrity of drywall mud

Cardio-adjacent.

Spiritually fulfilling.

The Cruella Coffee

Morning smelled like hope.

It looked like chaos.

Pans sizzled.

Steam drifted like incense.

A double boiler the size of a baptismal font sat on the stove.

"What'cha makin'?" I asked.

"A surprise for you, Signore."

She lifted the lid, checked the thermometer, then dangled a single coffee bean on a string into a steaming mug.

She counted.

"One-thousand one… one-thousand ten… and one-half."

The bean touched water for exactly 105 seconds.

Lecture mode activated.

"Steam gently heats. No scorching. All civilized."

She steamed my water and let one bold roast bean briefly share its essence.

It tasted like a rumor of caffeine.

I thanked her out loud

and whispered, "Cruella," into the mug.

Day Off (Training & Quiet)

Mulligan and Farah trotted in.

"Patrón," he said, "we request a day off. Farah has lessons with Jacqueline. She is feeling... full... around the middle."

"Enjoy yourselves," I said—already hearing the quiet of the drive ahead like a benediction.

Emotional Support Larry

At the funeral home, Larry greeted me on all fours.

He wore:

- a simulated retriever fur suit
- a matching tail
- a new ID tag reading: EMOTIONAL SUPPORT LARRY

"Maybe drive the flower car today," I offered gently.

"I ruv rlowers," he said.

"Is that... Scooby-Doo?"

"Ruh-Roh!"

Fa leaned in. "I brought him a dog-treat bowl. Also, Rabbi Jonathan called. 'The Director, The Priest, and The Chef' require tailor-made bulletproof vests."

"Let me guess," I said. "Two o'clock."

She blinked. "How'd you know?"

"Gift," I said.

Project Eliana (Reception Hall)

Where culinary fantasy collides with funeral reality

Two eighteen-wheelers idled behind the funeral home.

Inside, bubble wrap drifted like ticker tape over stainless-steel tables.

A clipboard read:

MAISON CULINAIRE — PROJECT ELIANA

Installed or in final wrapping:

- La Cornue Château 150 range
  - brass trim everywhere
  - the kind of stove you marry royalty to afford
- Miele speed + steam ovens
  - AI "soufflé therapy" mode
  - mood recognition (unfortunate)
- Sub-Zero glass-front columns
  - for heirloom lettuces
  - and post-service finger sandwiches
- Scotsman Nugget Ice Machine — Funeral Edition
  - soft enough for tears (joy or sorrow)
- Jura GIGA Espresso Temple
  - dual hoppers
  - sixteen programmable sermons
  - oat-milk frother ordained for duty
- Hestan copper-core cookware
  - engraved: TH&C
- Riedel crystal
  - "for sparkling water, tea, and respectful champagne"

Subtotal: $78,110

Honestly… lower than expected.

Then Fa handed me the next sheet.

The Signature Preparation Suite

Lemon-linen air.

Surgical precision.

More stainless steel than NASA.

Eliana supervised in a white coat like a Michelin-starred archangel.

New installation included:

- elite embalming machine
- Carrara marble hydraulic table
- HydroShield antimicrobial walls
- microbe-resistant ceiling
- chemical-proof flooring
- air system (ten changes per hour)
o signature scent: lemon-linen freshness
- surgical lighting array
- hands-free deep sinks
- RO/DI water system
- QuietRail mini lift
- walk-in cooler
- negative-pressure monitor
- VOC sensors
- wall-mounted smart tablet
o I'm convinced it already knew my mother's maiden name

Equipment subtotal: $197,100

Commissioned total: $232,200

Paid in full

Before I could process that, Nessun Dorma drifted in.

A stainless altar on wheels approached like the Ark of the Covenant.

EternaBot 10.

"It embalm-bathes-disinfects-dresses," the tech said proudly.

"Humidity control, thirty-minute resets, two complimentary opera tracks."

The bot:

- set faucets to 98.6°F
- folded towels into origami swans
- cleaned in figure-eights
- emitted a lavender glow
- purred in sync with the air unit

"How much?" I asked.

"Three-and-a-half million retail.

But $1.995M for a Texas field test."

I nodded like a man greeting a polite tornado.

Let me think about that.

(Not.)

Versailles on Wheels — The Florist Dock

At the florist, the loading dock looked like Versailles was relocating:

- lilies
- roses
- sprays requiring ladders
- wreaths the size of tractor tires

They were too busy creating beauty to babysit me, so I slipped away.

The Garden of Legacy

Where a funeral becomes a pilgrimage

At the cemetery, two hundred workers moved with the speed of unsupervised righteousness.

No bosses in sight—hence the progress.

In days, they had carved out an entire private section.

Lavender trembled in the breeze.

Design features restored and expanded:

- white-marble fountain
- bronze figure planned (arms open, serene)
- curved walkways spiraling inward
- limestone mini-amphitheater
- wrought-iron crest gates
- discreet speakers offering Pavarotti or Willie Nelson

The foreman promised Friday completion.

Standing there, I felt it.

If Saturday's dog wedding aimed for Wedding of the Century—

Friday's service was quietly becoming its equal.

The Funeral of the Century.

Lemon-Linen Benediction

By the time I reached my car, my budget had bruises—but my hair smelled faintly of lemon-linen purity.

"Talking Dog $20," I said to the windshield,

"I'm leaning toward a great decision."

Tomorrow:

- vest fittings at two (of course)
- a reception tasting where the soufflé AI wants to "speak with me privately"
- and one question no invoice answers:

What happens…

when the twelfth dove actually lands?

Chapter 31 — Vest, Gin, and Rug-Beating

The tailor had just finished chalking my initials into a swatch of Kevlar—right over my heart, the irony not lost on either of us—when I decided the day owed me something in exchange for emotional turbulence.

If Heaven, Rome, and the Rabbi all wanted me to be bulletproof, I figured I was entitled to stop by the club for a Butterfinger.

Worst case: Cheez-Its, honey-roasted peanuts, or chips made of ingredients you shouldn't read.

Best case: a game of dominoes, a few hands of gin, or a hamburger I didn't need and fully intended to order.

Inside, the guys were already camped out like aging philosophers—cards in hand, opinions fully formed.

"Day off?" one of them asked.

"Sort of," I said. "Got fitted for a tuxedo you can't stab."

They nodded, as if this explained everything.

I tried a few of my usual one-liners.

Polite chuckles all around.

Then one of them, without looking up from his cards, said,

"Mulligan's jokes are better."

"From a dog?" I asked.

He shrugged. "From that dog."

Fair.

I accepted my defeat with a side of Cheez-Its and the hamburger I'd promised myself I wouldn't order, then headed home—where the house had slipped into its usual Hallmark glow: soft music, too many throw blankets, and a level of contentment I'm still learning to accept.

Tomorrow, the gauntlet would begin.

The Morning of Consequence

Wednesday dawned with Eliana in full culinary command—pots singing, steam rising, everything smelling like discipline.

She slid a breakfast plate in front of me.

It tasted like vitamins, penitence, and one long French whisper: Behave.

"I'm going to the swing room," I announced.

This was only half a lie.

According to Mundo—loving friend, noted critic—my golf swing looked like I was beating a rug on a front porch in 1958.

He had named me Rug Beater, and I had since vowed to un-rug-beat myself.

On the stairs, Bella floated past like an Italian apparition—black dress, white gloves, heels that violated multiple OSHA standards.

"Buongiorno," I said.

She touched her fingers to her lips, offered a tiny blessing, and glided away.

Somewhere between the laundry room and the linen closet, she had discovered my hidden snack stash.

I didn't ask.

In the swing room, I performed my personal brand of cardio:

- a few Hogan swings
- a dozen putts into a coffee cup
- and a ham-and-cheese from the mini-fridge

"I'm a grown man," I whispered, "and I should be able to eat anything I want"—quietly enough that Eliana wouldn't materialize like an avenging angel.

When training hour concluded, I headed upstairs.

Mission Briefing

"Mulligan. Farah," I called. "Time to saddle up. We're needed."

Mulligan appeared, adjusting his Hogan cap with military precision.

Farah drifted in behind him like a silk curtain being unveiled in slow motion.

"Today," I said, "I'm on bodyguard duty. You two are emotional-support and spiritual-calming at the Rabbi's office. Tight schedule. Big day. Try not to outperform me too loudly."

Mulligan gave a crisp nod.

"Understated excellence," he said. "Our specialty."

Farah touched her nose to my hand—blessing, encouragement, or mild correction. Impossible to know.

I grabbed my keys, patted the pocket where a tailor had assured me I could now absorb small-caliber disagreements, and took a breath.

"Alright, team," I said.

"Let's go keep the peace—quietly."

We stepped into the morning like we meant it.

Chapter 32 — Knuckles, Blanks, and the Medal of Deniability

When we arrived at the fortified estate belonging to Jefe / The Rabbi / Jonathan / Señor International Man of Mystery, the guard waved us through with the urgency usually reserved for ambulances—or pizza deliveries on Super Bowl Sunday.

Jonathan met us at the door like a man hosting a charity gala for chaos.

"You're late," he said cheerfully, which is always how trouble starts.

He ushered us into a room occupied by a tattoo artist who looked like he sharpened his needles on motorcycle chains. A toy poodle sat in his lap, vibrating with enough suppressed rage to power a small city.

The poodle barked like a trumpet solo in a marching band.

Mulligan answered with three crisp barks—canine for *Know your place, small one.*

The poodle folded like a lawn chair.

"Ready for your knuckle tattoos, Director?" the tattoo man asked.

"I'm not getting a tattoo."

Jonathan waved a dismissive hand. "He's a wimp. Permanent marker. Standard protocol for temporary bodyguards."

"Temporary what?" I asked.

Ignored.

"Needles, go ahead."

Needles McGraw—best tattoo artist this side of Weatherford—grinned, uncapped a marker, and in thirty seconds made a decision that would haunt me at both the Funeral of the Century and the Wedding of the Millennium.

LAST CALL

stared back at me from my knuckles like I'd been promoted at a biker bar.

"I serve families," I protested. "I wear a suit. I am not a man who has Last Call on his knuckles."

Jonathan clapped me on the back.

"You are now. Don't worry—makeup will fix it. Probably."

Before I could object further, he shoved an AK-47 into my hands.

"Yours has blanks," he said. "Everyone else has live rounds."

"Oh good," I said. "I'm the warning shot while they're the consequences."

Even Barney Fife had one bullet.

Jonathan winked. "Leadership is about balance."

Jonathan's Curriculum for Criminal Continuing Education

He swept me through the estate and into a lineup of seminars no one had requested:

- Rebranding Kidnapping as Community Outreach
- How to Look Innocent in Photos
- Money Laundering 2.0: Apps That Won't Turn You In
- Mock Trial: Crying on Cue
- Smuggling for Beginners: The Dignified Waddle
- Poolside Karaoke — Don't Stop Believin' (Unless Federal Agents Appear)

Educational? Yes.

Legal? Absolutely not.

Denial? Already in practice.

The Banquet

The hall filled with enough questionable characters to populate a season of Narcos. I held my AK like Barney Fife wishing for permission to load his one bullet.

Then my brother stepped forward to bless the meal.

Father Ben's Cassock — A Family Legend

He wore the cassock—the one with a story stitched into every seam.

When he graduated from the seminary in Rome, our mother wanted something worthy of the moment. She marched into Sartoria Vaticana di Bellarmino & Figli, the oldest clerical tailor in Rome—a shop where:

- cassocks are cut like Renaissance paintings,
- every stitch is whispered over, and
- Massimo Bellarmino IV—eccentric as a peacock with a theology degree—insists that "a cassock must rustle with the sound of forgiveness."

Our mother told him,

"My son will serve families with compassion. Make him something holy enough to stand beside grief."

Massimo placed a hand over his heart.

"Madonna mia… I will sew him a miracle."

And he did.

Father Ben stepped to the podium in that miracle, and the room fell reverently silent. He made the Sign of the Cross. The cassock rustled—a soft, sacred whisper, like the turning of a Bible page.

His blessing rolled across the hall like incense.

"Benedicat vos Omnipotens Deus…"

It was gentle.

Simple.

Clean.

Even the toughest men blinked hard.

Mulligan whispered to Farah,

"Write that down. We're using it in our vows."

Enter: La Cofradía del Agave Negro

Then—she arrived.

La Cofradía didn't walk into the room.

She descended.

A tequila-fueled vision wrapped in smoke and sequins:

- Hair styled like a Category 3 hurricane
- Agave-leaf mariachi jacket
- Rosary of miniature tequila bottles
- Obsidian heels carved with cherubs fighting skeletons
- Eyebrows sharp enough for airport security
- Lips: radioactive lime green
- Nails painted with portraits of herself performing miracles
- Aura: danger, citrus, and questionable receipts

She lit a cigarillo with a spark from her fingernail.

"El Jefe," she purred. "I arrived before dinner. I simply came by a more interesting route."

Mulligan murmured,

"Farah, that goes in the vows too."

The Medal of Deniability

Awards followed:

- Clean Hands

- Best New Front (Tía Rosa's Nail & Bail)
- Most Improved Henchman (stopped texting during raids)
- Innovation in Smuggling (therapy dogs—Mulligan refuses comment)

Then came the summit award.

THE MEDAL OF DENIABILITY

Awarded to the one person everyone fears—yet no one can legally prove exists.

The winner:

La Cofradía del Agave Negro

A woman so elusive she exists legally as a weather event in Mexico.

Drones released añejo-scented rose petals as a mariachi rendition of O Fortuna thundered through the hall.

She raised the medal, smirked, and said,

"If anyone asks—I wasn't here, and neither was he."

The Toast — and the Miracle

Eliana emerged with a matte-black bottle labeled:

BUENAMORINE — For Mercy. For Memory.

Before a glass was poured, Father Ben stepped forward again. He placed a hand above the bottle and prayed—not loudly, not theatrically—but with the same quiet authority he uses beside grieving families.

The air shifted.

The lights softened.

The cassock whispered.

Even the drones hovered respectfully.

When La Cofradía took her sip—

She froze.

Her eyes softened first.

Then her jaw.

Her shoulders fell.

Her breath caught.

"I… have been unkind," she whispered.

"I have kept ledgers where there should have been lilies."

You could hear a rose petal land.

She cupped Jonathan's face.

"From this night forward, I repay what is owed, shield what is fragile, and protect what is sacred. Consider me your sword… and your worst enemy's plumber."

A collective exhale swept the hall.

Father Ben closed his eyes, satisfied.

Mulligan nodded, spiritually endorsing the moment.

Farah wiped a tear with her scarf.

Closing the Ledger

Later, in the library, she whispered to Jonathan,

"No more ledgers written in ink only the moon can read."

He promised.

At least for tonight.

I looked at my hands.

LAST CALL still glared back.

"Please," I whispered to no one, "let this makeup work tomorrow."

The air held the faint scent of rose, orange, and something that felt very much like forgiveness.

Chapter 33 — The Rooms of Miracles (and Mild Panic)

I woke after a few hours of sleep that felt like someone had pressed Skip Intro on my night. Mulligan and Farah stretched in unison—like synchronized swimmers who sleep in fur coats—then hopped down, alert and ready.

"Big day," I told them.

Mulligan nodded, as if he'd already read the itinerary.

In the kitchen, Eliana stood at full attention in pristine chef whites, her hair pinned up like a culinary general.

"I made breakfast burritos for everyone," she said sweetly. Then, with a pointed look, added,

"And one for you, Patrón. Not two. Don't test me."

We inhaled them. Mulligan ate his like a man facing execution at noon.

Arrival at the Funeral Home

When we pulled up, the scene looked like The Godfather met a quinceañera and invited The Oscars.

Flower vans.

Security teams.

Catering sprinters.

Event decorators with clipboards and the confidence of people who have never once been told no.

A guard stopped me at the door until Mulligan lifted his Service Dog badge—and added a soft growl for punctuation.

Inside, I spotted Larry.

Shaved.

Suit pressed.

Not just any suit—it shimmered like it had been woven from rescued shelter dogs.

"I wanted to look nice for the important people today," he said proudly.

A few Scooby-Doo syllables escaped him.

"Rorry... Mulligan's givin' me trainin' now. No more shock collars."

I patted his shoulder. "Proud of you, buddy."

Farah leaned in and whispered, "I think he really is part hound."

The Rooms

(Or: What Happens When Decorators Reach God-Tier)

The day before, the Cruz family's decorator said they would make "a few adjustments" to our Williamsburg and Sheridan Rooms.

Fine.

I can handle a floral arch.

Maybe new lighting.

What I walked into instead was this:

Mexico's cultural soul and a cathedral got married—and had twins.

Fa had texted me photos, but nothing prepared me for seeing it in person.

La Sala de Recuerdos — The Room of Remembrance

Warm amber lighting.

Marigolds cascading like a floral waterfall.

Devotional candles flickering in soft rows.

Papel picado dancing gently in the air.

A carved ofrenda altar so breathtaking I nearly left myself a thank-you note.

El Salón de Herencia — The Heritage Salon

Jewel-toned serapes.

Talavera pottery glimmering like stained glass.

Pan dulce towers.

Café de Olla drifting through the room like aromatic heaven.

A children's "Notes for Abuela" table.

Bilingual allergy labels—which almost made me tear up from pure professional joy.

This wasn't décor.

It was devotion.

I whispered,

"How in the hell are they going to put my rooms back by Friday?"

Then, quieter,

"How in the hell did they do this in one night?"

The Visitation

The Cruz family arrived, moving with a dignity that softened the entire room.

Everyone felt it immediately.

This wasn't just a visitation.

It was a love story.

Eliana's buffet was flawless.

Mulligan translated condolences and kept the security detail calm.

Even Larry helped—without shedding or barking at clergy.

By three o'clock, I collapsed into my massage chair like a man who had personally founded civilization. When Eliana wasn't looking, I stole snacks off the prep tray.

Quality control.

Mulligan curled at my feet.

Farah stretched by the door.

For a moment, everything felt exactly right.

This, I thought, is what it means to serve a family well.

Mulligan murmured, "Ruv roo," and drifted off.

Enter the Cardinal

(and Twelve Miraculous Birds)

When I woke, the Cardinal had just arrived.

The family lit up—you would have thought the Pope himself had walked in.

He explained the lost dove had been found on Mount Everest, and all twelve were now safe with a priest here in Fort Worth.

"And," he added warmly,

"He is the brother of the man who owns this funeral home."

I froze.

So did Mulligan.

The Cardinal Meets Mulligan

As the Cardinal entered the room, he saw Mulligan standing guard—ears up, chest out, posture perfect.

He stared.

Then whispered, "Hello… Dog."

Mulligan snapped to attention.

"You said Dog. Is there a mission?"

The Cardinal blinked.

"A... what?"

"The code word," Mulligan said urgently. "Are we active? Are we live?"

I stepped in.

"He's very... service-oriented."

The Cardinal studied him closely.

"You look exactly like the dog who saved the Pope's funeral..."

Mulligan stiffened with pride.

"That depends. Which Pope?"

The Cardinal crossed himself—slowly.

"He even moves like him."

Mulligan trotted off toward the catering trays as if nothing unusual had occurred.

I stared at the Cardinal.

He stared at Mulligan.

We were all thinking the same thing.

Is this dog an international religious incident?

Closing the Day

Later, when the doves were settled and the family embraced the Cardinal with gratitude, I stood with Mulligan and reflected:

When we say God has a plan...

God has a plan.

And sometimes that plan includes

a talking dog,

a cultural masterpiece of a visitation,

and a Cardinal receiving classified intel

from someone who eats off a plate on the floor.

Chapter 34 — The Funeral of the Century

The drive home the night before felt different.

Mulligan sat in the back seat like a decorated admiral on leave.

Farah gazed at him with the calm pride of a queen whose knight had returned from battle without losing his collar.

I told him he'd done an outstanding job.

For once, he didn't correct me.

Farah shimmered with approval—though, to be fair, her resting expression already looks like praise carved by Michelangelo.

The house was quiet that night. Dinner passed without commentary. We watched Scooby-Doo in companionable silence. Mulligan said he needed to "work on his dialect to understand Larry better." Farah sighed—the sound of a duchess whose calendar exhausted her.

I mentioned I might go hit a few balls.

Bella stopped me with her signature look—one finger to her lips, one slow shake of the head, opera gloves shimmering.

I obeyed.

Morning

The next morning, Mulligan and Farah were already engaged in what they called Canine Calisthenics—For Peak Performance and Tail Control. They ate breakfast like Olympians.

I sipped my coffee like a man who suspected history was warming up outside.

Because today was the day.

The funeral of the century.

Arrival and Preparations

The funeral home looked less like a workplace and more like the staging ground for a presidential inauguration—directed by Netflix.

Crews everywhere.

Motor officers are arriving in formation.

Buses idling as if they were about to transport people to the Grammys.

Larry—bless him—stood proudly in a brown suit with black spots, inspired loosely by a Dalmatian and finished with a bolo tie that defied logic.

He now spoke exclusively in Scooby-Doo.

"Ruh-roh! Red-y, roll!"

I nodded as if fluent.

Fa leaned in. "We owe her reimbursement for dog biscuits. He ate the entire bag yesterday."

By eleven o'clock, the parking lot had become a symphony:

- Five executive buses
- Ten Sprinter vans
- Four limousines

All queued with military precision.

Mulligan stood at the center, clipboard in paw, calling roll like an air-traffic controller.

"Load last, first; first, last," he reminded everyone.

"This is the opposite of brisket service."

Then came the hum.

Eighteen motorcycle officers in perfect formation. Lights flashing. Boots polished.

One of them saluted Mulligan.

Mulligan winked.

I took a breath. "Alright, everyone. Let's make history."

Bass Hall

Bass Hall did not look like Bass Hall.

It looked like the moment before creation—air trembling with light, color, and expectation.

Four eighteen-wheelers of florals had been unloaded, yet every petal seemed placed by a single, reverent hand.

At the entrance stood The Archway of Angels—orchids, Oaxacan tuberose, moon-white lilies, and pearl-strung vines shimmering in the morning light. People approached it slowly, as if it were a relic.

Inside, the aisle had become The Garden of Remembrance—marigold, rose, bluebonnet, orchid—less a walkway than an invitation into someone's life.

At the front rose The Altar of Memory: lilies, proteas, roses, and hand-carved onyx engraved with prayers. Soft amber light haloed everything it touched. For a moment, everyone looked as though heaven had already noticed them.

And the music—

André Rieu's violin drifted through the hall. Strings from Vienna and Prague warmed the air. Harps tuned in crystalline waves.

It sounded like wings stretching before flight.

The dignitaries gathered:

- Cardinal Esteban de la Vega of Guadalajara
- The Bishops of Fort Worth and Dallas
- Paloma del Río — La Voz del Corazón
- Don Rafael Castillo-Ortiz — Patron of the Arts
- Dr. Lucía Herrera Cortés — National Poet Laureate

And inexplicably:

A beach chair.

An umbrella.

A small cooler.

"For Father Ben," the stagehand whispered. "Moral support. He insisted."

Only in my life could a man prepare for the holiest service imaginable and still require SPF 100.

Mulligan surveyed the splendor and whispered, tail flicking once:

"Subtle."

The universe felt balanced again.

The Service

At two o'clock sharp, the doors opened.

Incense rose.

Mulligan entered first—steady, solemn, a service dog in full ceremonial bearing.

Father Ben followed, sunscreen in hand.

Then the bishops.

The Cardinal.

Twelve Texas Rangers in full dress uniform.

Between them, the gold-plated casket glinted beneath soft white light.

Behind it all, the Cruz family—wrapped in faith, courage, and gentle tears.

The orchestra moved into "Nearer, My God, to Thee."

The hall breathed as one.

Cardinal de la Vega lifted his hands.

"Hoy no lloramos la ausencia, sino celebramos la presencia eterna del amor."

Today we do not weep for absence but celebrate love's eternal presence.

The Garden of Legacy

The cemetery was no longer a burial ground—it was a cathedral of open sky.

At its heart stood a three-tiered marble fountain carved in Florence, crowned by La Testigo—The Witness—a figure holding heaven and home in equal measure.

Seven winding gardens spiraled outward like a living rosary: lavender, roses, bluebonnets, tulips, marigolds, hydrangeas, jasmine.

Wind chimes tuned to E-flat—her favorite key—rang softly in the breeze.

The limestone amphitheater waited.

One hundred beagles inhaled in perfect unison.

Gregorian chant, by way of pure canine devotion.

People wept openly.

Someone whispered, "Heaven sounds like this."

Then the air shimmered.

From the fountain's mist emerged memory—her garden, her kitchen, her laughter, her love—each moment carrying its own scent.

"Mamá… estás aquí," one daughter whispered.

Even Mulligan's eyes glistened.

The Doves

Twelve white doves rose into the sky, circling once.

One climbed higher.

"La Primera," the Cardinal whispered.

And for a breath of time, light shaped itself into a smile.

A blessing.

Reflections

That night, exhausted in my chair, I thought about everything.

Talking dog: twenty dollars.

French Afghan: five thousand.

Funeral of the century: beyond calculation.

Helping a family heal—priceless.

Mulligan curled beside Farah and whispered,

"Patrón… we did well today."

He was right.

We did.

Chapter 35 — Something Borrowed, Something Blue (and Ten Sky-Trackers)

I let the entire kennel—canine and human—sleep in and slipped out to the funeral home alone.

For the first time in living memory, Larry wasn't camped on the front step. Fa waved from behind the desk and said he'd called in about "getting his tux."

Good, I thought.

He is renting a tux.

Progress.

I walked through the building the way Dad used to—hands clasped behind my back—listening to the place breathe.

The Williamsburg and Sheridan Rooms didn't just look restored; they looked renewed, as if Dad himself had set down his polishing cloth thirty seconds before I arrived.

How did they do that in one night? I wondered.

Then again… how did they do it the other night?

In the chapel, florists were giving yesterday's grandeur a second bow. Reused arrangements usually wilt fast—except these hadn't. They stood taller, fuller, as if the flowers themselves knew who was coming down the aisle.

Down the hall, EternaBot 10 hummed in neat figure eights, buffing marble with the earnest determination of an overachieving Roomba auditioning for sainthood.

"What's that robot still doing here?" I asked Fa.

"Elon said we should test it for a month," she replied. "He'll pick him up if we don't want to keep him."

"It's him?"

She shrugged. "He answers to Bleep."

Outside, a rental crew positioned ten sky-trackers, their beams already rehearsing for nightfall—clean white lines slicing the Texas sky like promises being underlined.

Inside, the Beagle Choir warmed up: long vowels, respectable blend, one optimistic tenor in the back who would be spoken to later.

In the kitchen, Eliana was already at work on what she referred to as the Royal Wedding Feast.

"Whatcha makin'?" I asked.

The look she gave suggested I consult the menu rather than her patience.

I did—and then made the tactical mistake of reading the dog menu.

Hunger became philosophical.

I briefly considered ordering the Surf & Turf à la Paw for myself and pleading confusion.

Getting Ready

By afternoon, the house had traded last night's Hallmark serenity for disciplined chaos.

Mulligan showed the faintest signs of nerves.

I knelt, placed a hand on his chest, and felt the steady percussion of his heart.

"Relax, buddy," I said. "It's happening. Go with the flow."

He inhaled once—deeply—the way people do when they decide to trust the moment—then nodded.

Farah blinked serenely, already composed, already regal. A queen who had approved the seating chart days ago.

Then Julia descended the stairs.

Her gown—French-lavender silk chiffon over satin—moved like whispered music. Silver-lilac beadwork traced the bateau neckline. Pearls glowed at her throat; diamond teardrops caught the light. A soft fascinator framed her hair just enough to suggest Paris without alarming Fort Worth.

Her nosegay—gardenias, violets, a single gold-dusted orchid—rested easily in her hand.

Champagne pumps said blessing first, dancing later.

She was dignity with a heartbeat.

Farah pressed her head into that lavender skirt like a child greeting her mother.

It was the gentlest moment of the day.

And it was not even close.

Eliana appeared next in amethyst satin, calm and luminous—the sort of woman who could manage a kitchen or a kingdom without raising her voice.

Jacqueline swept in as Maid of Honor: charcoal-blue silk, halter neckline, angel-wing comb placed just so. Gloves that signaled peacekeeping authority.

Bella followed, poured into liquid black satin, pearls gleaming, a single white gardenia pinned like absolution. Her perfume arrived five seconds before she did and was likely illegal in at least three countries.

Anna Belle arrived in blush-and-ivory tulle, her petal-propulsion harness hidden beneath couture engineering.

Teddy wore an ivory vest with gold piping, carrying Farah's collar on a silk cushion like a miniature viscount who took his duties seriously.

I adjusted my old tux—it still fit, mostly—and counted heads.

Not enough seats.

Mulligan cleared his throat.

"I rented a limo for the ladies. After the reception, Eliana and Bella are going to a country bar to pick up cowboys."

"The Cowboys are out of town," I said.

"Not those Cowboys," he replied. "Cowboy cowboys."

You can't make that up.

Except they could.

The Grand Entrances

We pulled into the lot beneath ten sky-trackers combing the Fort Worth night like searchlights for joy—or rescue, depending on who you asked. The beams crossed and uncrossed above the chapel roof, slow and deliberate, as if the sky itself were being checked for credentials.

I stopped Mulligan at the door.

"To my office, sir. It isn't appropriate to see your bride before the wedding."

He straightened, adjusted an invisible cuff, and pivoted like a gentleman burglar disappearing down a hallway he already knew too well.

"Patrón," he called back softly, "Farah still needs something borrowed and something blue."

That tone—the one he used when he knew something—gave me pause.

I fetched Julia's mother's lace handkerchief and a narrow French-blue silk ribbon. Jacqueline stitched and wove with surgical calm. When she clipped the tiny sapphire charm into Farah's collar, it caught the light once—then went still, like it had found its place.

Then the doors opened.

The first arrivals came quietly.

Too quietly.

Men in tailored black coats moved through the lobby with spacing you only see where people have learned not to bunch—security details, old funerals, diplomatic corridors. They nodded to one another, not friendly, not cold—acknowledgment without curiosity.

One paused at the stained glass. "Original," he murmured.

"Restored," another replied without looking up. "Faithfully."

I didn't remember telling anyone that.

Then Larry arrived.

The door swung open and the room changed temperature. The Beagle Choir lost pitch for half a second.

Larry stepped inside dressed like a man who had once been important, forgotten it, and decided to remember.

Jet-black tux. Shawl collar. Paw-print studs. Bone-shaped bow tie. Jacket tails—with an actual tail. Cowboy boots etched with dog bones. White rose boutonniere. Midnight felt hat with a retriever-fur band.

He posed.

"Rello, rirector."

The lobby applauded. Somewhere, a Beagle hit a high C.

Larry tipped his hat and stepped aside.

Then they arrived.

The Gentlemen of His Holiness entered not as a group, but as a sequence. Tailcoats. White gloves. Cross-keys pins that flashed only when the light wanted them to.

Their Papal Stetsons came off in unison.

I'd heard Mulligan's stories—wild ones—about Rome, about funerals that shut down cities, about men who stood watch over grief like sentinels.

I told myself this was a coincidence.

One of them glanced toward the chapel and murmured, "This will do."

That should have bothered me more than it did.

Then came Mulligan's old friends.

You noticed the men second.

They moved like people who understood silence as a language and exits as optional. Two—Vex and Havoc—shook my hand gently. Too gently. Like they were reminding themselves this evening had rules.

Their dogs stepped forward first. No frenzy. No sniffing. Just assessment.

Introductions happened without sound.

Then Farah's friends arrived.

Silk. Satin. Heels that knew how to land softly.

Dogs held like accessories—but the dogs themselves were not accessories. They moved with recognition, with memory.

Bella. Coco. Giselle.

Owners smiled and shook hands because that's what people do.

The dogs leaned in close and settled—like soldiers recognizing a familiar unit. Like family confirming no one was missing.

I caught myself thinking, These people flew here.

Then I realized the truth.

The dogs did.

Ben Rubin arrived with his group in their best golf attire. I handed him a cigar box.

"Your favorites," I said. "From Mulligan, with apologies."

He paused. "He remembered."

Mundo tipped his cap. "Hello, Rug Beater."

Hogan's niece hugged my neck. "Ben would have loved this."

Ian Anderson Cousteau lifted a silver flute and let one line of Debussy drift through the lobby like a promise.

Elon Musk appeared, complimented my dog, asked about the robot, and was gently redirected.

The Cardinal arrived slightly winded. "That twelfth dove tried to escape again."

The Richardsons entered carrying a Bible.

The French Ambassador bowed deeply.

Gordon Ramsay sniffed and cornered Eliana. "Soufflé?"

"No," she said. "Joy that won't fall."

A nurse approached with a rosary. "I met Mulligan in Mexico," she said. "He sat with a woman who had forgotten everything—except her daughter's name."

Then the Rabbi arrived in a Bentley, handed Mulligan the keys, and said, "You won this. It's yours."

Fa swept in with a clipboard that could end nations.

Espresso drifted through the chapel like incense with a culinary degree.

Security broke up a disagreement in pew twelve involving two bulldogs and theology.

The Bishop of Dallas slipped into the transept.

I checked my watch.

7:55.

Showtime.

And for the first time—just briefly—I wondered if Mulligan hadn't been making things up at all.

Chapter 36 — Doors Lights Breath

The Great Transfiguration of the Chapel

By sunset, the Sheridan Chapel no longer looked like a chapel.

It looked like the wedding planners of

- ✨ the Vatican,
- ✨ Broadway,
- ✨ a royal coronation,
- ✨ and a Las Vegas headliner show

had all shared one Google calendar by accident—and nobody dared cancel.

Ten sky-trackers swept the Fort Worth sky like beacons announcing the birth of a new constellation. Laser projections danced across the roofline in lavender, gold, and sapphire—Farah's colors—so vivid the building seemed to glow from the inside out.

Florals arched over every doorway: cascading orchids, Persian violets, white roses dusted with edible shimmer, and Arabian jasmine woven into constellations of scent.

Inside, the pews glowed beneath soft amber light. Stained-glass projections shimmered across the walls—Saint Francis, Saint Roch, Moses, Ruth—each reimagined with a faithful dog at their side like a theological Easter egg.

Across the front wall, a custom mural hovered in gentle light:

LOVE IS LOYALTY MADE VISIBLE

Painted by candlelight by an artist who cried the entire time.

The Beagle Choir—one hundred strong and freshly groomed—sat in perfect formation in an amphitheater loft built for this night only. DJ Shlomo B adjusted his turntables reverently, wearing a yarmulke stitched with tiny musical notes. The GSF Organ Ensemble warmed their pipes as if tuning for the Second Coming.

Everything hummed with expectation.

The Officiant Summit

In my office, Father Ben and Rabbi Jonathan stood over the wedding program like generals preparing an invasion.

They reviewed choreography:

- Holy water in a clockwise blessing arc
- Kosher broth in a counter-clockwise splash
- Unity sprinkle-broth crossfade
- Four-part benediction with optional organ swell

"Gentlemen," I said, "this is ecclesiastical diplomacy at its finest."

They fist-bumped.

It was going to be that kind of night.

The Prelude — A Full-Scale Symphonic Warm-Up

The lights dimmed.

Candles flared.

A low golden hum ran the length of the chapel, as if the building itself were taking a breath.

Prélude setlist:

- La Vie en Rose — string quartet
- How Great Thou Bark — pipe organ with trumpet descant
- Hava Nagila (Paw Mix) — DJ Shlomo B remix with klezmer clarinet

The Beagle Choir contributed harmonic under-paws.

Complimentary biscuits under pew two were removed after two bulldogs attempted to claim them as sovereign territory.

The Processional — A Royal Parade of Paws & People

Anna Belle entered first to Walking on Sunshine. Her petal-propulsion harness—engineered by Elon Musk and Jacqueline—released a perfect trail of blush rose petals with the precision of NASA thrusters.

Teddy followed to Cheek to Cheek, carrying Farah's silk-nestled collar with ceremonial solemnity that rivaled yesterday's Texas Rangers.

Then—

The chapel drew breath.

Farah appeared.

A veil of shimmering desert silk. Baltic-crystal embroidery. A French-blue ribbon woven into her topknot. A single sapphire charm catching the light like a blessing in motion.

Escorted by Julia—radiant and poised—they glided forward to a fusion of Edith Piaf, Yo-Yo Ma, and a Beagle Choir hum that could convert atheists.

Finally—

Mulligan entered to Ain't That a Kick in the Head.

Tail low. Ears poised. Eyes bright with devotion…and mild panic.

I walked him halfway down the aisle.

"I'm your father?" I whispered.

"No," he replied. "But we can pretend until the photographs are done."

The Opening Rite — The Holy Duet

Father Ben raised the aspergillum.

Rabbi Jonathan raised the broth ladle.

They blessed the room in coordinated arcs—perfect figure-eights—so synchronized the audience gasped.

"This is better than Cirque du Soleil," Mulligan whispered.

Farah nodded regally.

The Readings — Sacred and Slightly Less Sacred

Genesis 2:18

It is not good for dog to be alone.

Psalm 23½

Thy stick and thy bone, they comfort me.

The Talmutt, Book of Puppers

Blessed is he who fetches faithfully.

People took pictures of that one.

The Homily — The Gospel of Good Boys

The lights softened. The organ murmured the first bars of What a Wonderful World.

Father Ben preached:

"Love is loyalty wrapped in fur."

Rabbi Jonathan preached:

"Covenant is choosing one another—every day."

Together:

"And kibble. Always kibble."

A bishop dabbed his eyes.

A bulldog dabbed its jowls.

The Vows — A Sacrament of Heart

Teddy stepped forward with perfect timing.

Father Ben and Rabbi Jonathan fastened the collar together—

one Christian hand,

one Jewish hand,

one sacred promise.

The room dissolved into joyful tears.

Even Larry sniffed loudly enough to echo.

The Unity Ceremonies — Symbolism and Snacks

The Kibble Candle

Two bowls became one crystal chalice.

Breaking of the Milk-Bone

Rabbi Jonathan cracked it cleanly.

DJ Shlomo B added a rimshot.

Farah laughed.

Mulligan beamed.

The Pronouncement — The Moment of Moments

Father Ben:

"By the power vested in us by Church, Synagogue, and Fort Worth Animal Control…"

Rabbi Jonathan:

"Mazel tov—you may now lick the bride!"

For one suspended second, nothing moved.

Not the choir.

Not the clergy.

Not even the dogs.

It was the kind of silence that only happens when everyone present understands—without instruction—that something irrevocable and good has just occurred.

Mulligan leaned his forehead gently against Farah's.

No flourish.

No joke.

Just gratitude.

In that held breath, every vow that had ever mattered in that room felt remembered.

Then the wings began.

Eleven white doves rose.

The twelfth—who knows where the twelfth was.

A grandmother fainted.

Two bishops applauded.

One Chihuahua ascended a pew.

The Recessional — A Festival of Light and Sound

Happy transitioned into Who Let the Dogs Out—

a choice we regretted immediately.

Anna Belle's harness detonated Confetti Mode: gold, lavender, white.

EternaBot 10 whispered "Bleep bleep" and polished every surface like a monk scrubbing relics.

Sky-trackers crossed overhead in X-formation, throwing cathedral beams across downtown Fort Worth.

Someone outside shouted,

"WHO IS GETTING MARRIED IN THERE—BEYONCÉ?"

No.

Better.

Mulligan and Farah.

The Reception — A Feast for the Ages

Eliana's banquet was culinary diplomacy at its peak.

Twin cakes arrived—one human, one canine.

Silver bowls clinked like champagne.

At 12:15 a.m., the Beagle Choir performed Can't Help Falling in Love.

At 1:45, bishops nodded approvingly to Ave Maria.

At 2:00, the sky-trackers blinked a gentle goodbye.

Fort Worth had hosted a miracle.

The Final Moment — Love, Quiet, Light

Later, the chapel finally stilled.

Julia.

Fa.

Eliana.

Jacqueline.

Bella.

Father Ben.

Rabbi Jonathan.

And me.

Mulligan rested his head on Farah's shoulder. Her sapphire charm—something blue—glowed.

"Patrón," he whispered, "did we do okay?"

I looked at the radiant chaos—the florals, the candles, Larry tipping his cowboy hat, the Pope's barista pulling one last macchiato—and nodded.

"You didn't just do okay," I said. "You made history."

Long after the lights dimmed and the last petal was swept away, the chapel would still remember.

Wood always does.

Walls do.

And if you listened closely—very closely—some nights you could swear the place exhaled.

As if it knew what had happened there.

As if it had been waiting.

As I locked up and stepped into the cool night air, I caught sight of the old sign in my mind — the one that never quite hangs straight.

We treat people like family.

A little crooked.

A little imperfect.

Still true.

Dad used to say if a place looks too polished, people won't trust it. Grief needs room to lean. Love does too.

Tonight had been flawless — lights, music, miracles, even doves with altitude problems.

But that sign reminded me why it all mattered.

Because at the end of the night, after the sky-trackers power down and the choirs go home, what people remember isn't the spectacle.

They remember whether they were cared for.

I straightened my jacket, left the sign crooked where it belonged, and turned off the lights.

Chapter 37 — The Morning After

The morning after the wedding rose slow and sideways—like the sun wasn't entirely sure it wanted to be responsible for whatever it was about to reveal.

The Kitchen

Eliana moved across the kitchen like a documentary on the migration of wounded animals. She wore a midnight felt hat with a yellow-white silk band and a tiny crossed-keys pin—the formal hat of the Gentlemen of His Holiness. Or, apparently, the Gentlewomen.

"Morning," I said gently.

"Why are you yelling?" she croaked.

"I'm not yelling."

"Stop yelling."

I opened the cabinet, removed the Alka-Seltzer, and shook it gently like communion.

Her hands trembled as she accepted it. "Bless you," she whispered.

Anna Belle and Teddy sprawled nearby—heads low, eyes glassy—like underage freshmen who'd snuck into the homecoming punch. Teddy's silk vest was now less vest and more suggestion.

"I'm not hungry," I announced, patting my stomach for courage and finding none. "I'm going to hit a few balls."

Bella Appears

Halfway down the stairs, Bella intercepted me—sweats, tennis shoes, hair in a long-term negotiation with gravity.

"You speak English," I said.

"Only when my head feels like this," she replied, rubbing her temples. "And if I'm gonna keep coverin' for you sneakin' food and vodka down here, I want a raise."

She paused.

"Nice hat. Looks like the one Larry had on last night."

Her eyes slid sideways—mischief, memory, and regret braided together.

Larry... oh my.

A Brief and Ineffective Practice Session

My "practice" consisted of five swings, two breakfast bars, and a cup of actual coffee with actual cream.

Ben Hogan disapproved from Heaven.

Rug Beater approved from Hell.

Julia

Upstairs, Julia stood at the window, framed by soft light and last night's magic—her smile still tethered to the ceremony.

"Wasn't that the most beautiful wedding you've ever seen?" she whispered.

She didn't turn. She didn't need to.

"It was perfect," she said. "Even Mulligan looked handsome."

"Kinda," I whispered, kissing her cheek.

For a moment, the house felt holy—not loud-holy, just quietly intact.

The Scene of the Celebration

The funeral home looked like a cathedral that had survived a Mardi Gras hurricane.

Larry

Larry was still in his tux—creased, wrinkled, heroic in defeat. His Scooby-Doo dialect was now being filtered through a desert-dry hangover.

"Where's your hat, Larry?"

He blinked twice. Once per hemisphere.

Oh my.

Bella… what did you do?

Fa and the Situation Report

Fa intercepted me with a clipboard, hair pinned like she had climbed out of a tornado and decided to organize it.

"I hired a cleaning crew and told 'em to bring extra of everything," she said. "This place looks and smells like a party, a pound, and rotten food had a baby."

She wasn't wrong.

The Cigar Box

In the reception hall, Ben Rubin's cigar box sat open on the counter—a peace offering. A pledge of reconciliation.

I lifted the lid.

It was… a crime scene.

Someone had peed—precisely, surgically—on the end of every cigar except one.

A statement of diplomacy.

And bladder control.

The Cappuccino Potato

Nearby sat a cappuccino cup, half-full, foam art intact.

It wasn't a flower.

It wasn't a leaf.

It was a potato.

A perfect little foam potato.

I set it down carefully—like evidence.

Incoming Calls

Fa stuck her head back in. "Phone again. French Foreign Legion commander. Still missing their man."

"Tell them nothing," I said. "Tell them everything. Tell them… he's probably in a bar."

Gordon Ramsay

In the kitchen, Gordon Ramsay was still there.

Still whisking.

Still muttering.

Still committing soufflé homicide.

"Chef… everything okay?"

He slammed the oven. "They fall—they always fall! This humidity is sabotage! Where's the beagle who ate my meringue?"

I backed away slowly. Carefully. Prayerfully.

The Aftermath and the Note

Fa returned with the urgency of a fire alarm, wearing a headset.

"Police are on the line. Diplomatic immunity. Passed out Bentley. Cowboy bar."

I blinked.

Of course.

Naturally.

Inevitable.

"They found a note," she said, handing it to me.

I read:

To Mulligan and Farah,

This Bentley is the least I could do for the most incredible couple on earth.

— Your devoted admirer, The Rabbi

I looked up.

"Better call the French president," I said. "We found their man."

The Chapel

Inside, the Gentlemen of His Holiness lay sprawled in symmetrical, holy disarray—like Renaissance cherubs who'd grown up, joined the clergy, and lost a battle with Tito's vodka.

Their snores harmonized—resonant, papal, nearly liturgical.

Somewhere, a brass section chimed in.

I chose to believe it was trumpets.

The Putting Green

Out back, three of the toughest dogs alive slept nose-to-nose with three show dogs—like peace had been negotiated at dawn by diplomats wearing rhinestone collars.

"I hope they're sleeping," I whispered.

The Robot and the Dove

In the reception hall, EternaBot 10 traced panicked figure-eights, steam hissing like an emotional-support kettle.

A lone dove perched atop the bone-broth fountain—exhausted, beatific, and mildly disappointed in all of us.

A Beginning in Disguise

I surveyed the battlefield:

- wilted florals
- glitter explosions
- a soufflé graveyard
- diplomats unconscious in automobiles
- a dove with secrets
- a robot having a nervous breakdown

And from down the corridor came the soft clatter of a leash—and Mulligan's voice, bright, awake, unstoppable:

"Patrón, good morning. We have… updates."

I took a breath.

Straightened my tie.

Looked around at the ruin, the beauty, and the absurdity.

In a house built for endings,

this morning felt suspiciously—

miraculously—

like a beginning.

Chapter 38 — The Best Decision I Ever Made

Within three weeks of the wedding, our little funeral home on Camp Bowie went global.

Families flew in asking for Mulligan to consult on funerals—and, thanks to the nuptials, on weddings and bar and bat mitzvahs too. We said yes to a few: a rainy-day wake in Dublin (indoors, no puddles), a garden wedding in Kyoto, a joyful bar mitzvah in Tel Aviv.

Mulligan traveled like he'd been doing it his whole life—calm, kind, and unnervingly precise about canapé ratios.

Meanwhile, something else happened that night at the annual banquet-that-does-not-like-being-named. Something unexpected.

After Doña Catrina changed her ways, the room chose Jonathan—Jefe to them, Rabbi to us—as the new leader. He raised a glass "to the sinister," paused, and had Eliana pour BuenAmorine for everyone.

Two hundred and fifty glasses.

The toast landed.

One by one, people renounced violence, poison, and profit from misery. They pledged treatment for addiction. Food for the hungry.

A week later, Oslo called.

Mulligan received the Nobel Peace Prize, which he insisted on calling the Nobel Piece Prize, "because peace is built piece by piece." He let a child in the front row hold the medal "to see how it feels."

That photo was everywhere by breakfast.

Back home, Farah began to show on day fifty—not that we were counting.

Labor started. Long. Hard. Three breech.

Julia held Farah's paw. I kept time. Mulligan stood so steady he hardly breathed.

Finally: twelve pups. Eleven tiny Farahs and one tiny Mulligan.

We made a warm half-moon around them and just listened to the squeaks.

By noon, the media had found us. Offers poured in—two hundred and fifty thousand dollars a puppy, and climbing.

That evening in the hallway, Mulligan sat beside me like a man finishing a rosary.

"Patrón," he said, "I love her. I love them. I never want her to be in pain like this again. I thought we were going to lose her. I'm getting fixed.

"And please—no auctions. We have a list of people we trust for our babies."

I closed the ledger and said, "Okay."

A few minor things settled into place.

One of the Gentlemen of His Holiness asked to stay—because he'd fallen in love with Eliana. We suited him up as an Apprentice Funeral Director and enrolled him at the Dallas Institute of Funeral Service. He bows to families the way some men bow to altars.

Turns out, both are forms of reverence.

The Texas Funeral Service Commission stopped by with a framed certificate titled Mulligan, Honorary Canine Funeral Consultant (Texas) and a ribbon. He wore the ribbon for twelve minutes, then gave it to a kid "so he could feel official while he learned how to be kind."

Then came Puppy Day—quick, gentle, one family at a time:

- Rabbi Jonathan took Mercy and whispered, "For bread, not bullets."

- Father Ben blessed Benedict and smiled. "Confession available—probably unnecessary."

- Eliana accepted Biscotti and asked if kibble should be plated or framed.

- Bella took Luce and finally let herself grin.

- Jacqueline and Ian lifted Étoile and promised Dog French at dawn.

- Fa kissed Gracie and put a treat bowl at the reception desk.

- Larry, in his black tux and cowboy hat, met Scooby Doo and whispered, "Rello, Rcooby Roo," and the pup wagged like he already understood.

- Doña Catrina fastened Clemencia's collar. "No ledgers—only lilies."

- Mundo slung Rugger like a nine-iron. Fewer swings. More walks.

- Ben Rubinski received Cohiba with a little trepidation.

- Mrs. Cruz's granddaughter held Rosa and said, "For Abuela," and the room went quiet.

- We kept the little Mulligan twin and named him Hogan.

That night, the den felt like grace.

Julia with a blanket.

Eliana with popcorn she pretended not to salt.

The Gentleman of His Holiness beside her.

Bella on the armrest.

Larry on his knees, hands on the floor like a dog in training.

Anna Belle polite.

Teddy snoring.

Farah with a paw over Hogan.

Mulligan beside them all.

We put on Pick of the Litter—gentle, hopeful, the kind of story that knows how to end in a kitchen.

Halfway through the movie, Hogan—still wobbly, still smelling faintly of warm milk and miracles—climbed onto Mulligan's chest, planted his tiny paws, puffed himself up like a pocket-sized opera singer, and said, perfectly clearly:

"Da-Da."

Time stopped.

Not quiet—frozen.

Julia's hand flew to her mouth.

Bella gasped so loudly the Gentleman of His Holiness reflexively blessed the room.

Larry's cowboy hat slid clean off his head as he fainted.

Eliana spilled her popcorn.

Actual tears rose.

Even Teddy's snore hiccupped to a halt.

I whispered, "Did he… did he just say 'Da-Da'?"

Julia nodded, eyes enormous. "He did. He absolutely did."

Farah lifted her head, eyes glowing, voice trembling with wonder.

"He said 'Da-Da,'" she murmured, soft as a hymn. "Our baby said 'Da-Da.'"

Then—because this night still had one more miracle chambered—Anna Belle blinked and said, clear as Sunday sunshine:

"That's so cute!"

The room screamed again—because she was talking too.

I turned toward Teddy.

He cleared his throat like an old senator preparing remarks and said, "Rof rourse."

(Of course, in Teddy.)

Then added, matter-of-factly, "Re all can ralk."

Anna Belle nodded primly. "Mulligan has been teaching us," she said.

We humans sat there stunned—awed to silence, the way people react to shooting stars, first breaths, and answered prayers.

Mulligan looked around—part proud dad, part professor, part dog who knew something we didn't. His ears relaxed.

The room loosened into easy chatter. Questions. Answers. Opinions about popcorn salt. A brief debate on the ethics of squirrels.

Not noisy—alive.

From the end of the sofa, Eliana squeezed the hand of the Gentleman of His Holiness and looked across to Larry and Bella.

"Mulligan," she said, smiling through happy-tired eyes, "would you help us plan something?"

Larry straightened his cowboy hat.

Bella blushed.

The Gentleman bowed—old habits.

"A double wedding," Eliana said. "Bella and Larry. Me and—" She glanced at him.

"And me," the Gentleman finished softly.

Mulligan's ears tipped forward, amused and tender.

"Rehearsal at four, vows at five, cake at six," he said. "Papal bicornes optional. Cowboy hats encouraged."

The laughter that followed felt like a promise.

Mulligan let it settle, then turned to me with the last line ready.

"I told you, "He said. "I can teach a dog faster and better than any human."

I laughed until I teared up.

In a house built for endings, we'd become a classroom for beginnings.

Talking Dog $20—best decision I ever made.

Postscript (Tech Edition)

The next morning, a press release arrived from somewhere between Palo Alto and Mars.

Elon was partnering with "two extremely opinionated companies" to launch Southern Sorry—a voice assistant that says "ma'am" and "sir," tells you where the good pie is, and apologizes twice before setting a reminder.

On select phones, you'll say, "Hey, Sorry."

On certain speakers, "Leexa" (pending détente and a bake-off).

Mulligan read it, sighed happily, and said:

"Progress comes piece by piece—and sometimes with pie."

Acknowledgments

Writing this book has been one of the most joyful—and unexpected—adventures of my life.

To Janice—my compass, my calm, and the one who still laughs at my stories no matter how many times she's heard them None of this happens without you.

To Jon, for building on our family legacy with kindness, heart, and a deep respect for the people we serve Watching you carry it forward has been one of my greatest joys

To Father Tim, for reminding me that faith and humor are siblings, not strangers—and that laughter often opens doors prayer alone cannot.

To Martha (Fa), for always being there, for knowing what needs to be done before it's said out loud, and for being a twin in every way that matters.

To everyone at Thompson's Harveson & Cole Funeral Home and Martin Thompson & Son Funeral Home—thank you for living the ministry, not just doing the work Your compassion shows up when it matters most.

To my friends who pushed, polished, questioned, and encouraged this project—you know who you are, and this book is better because of you.

And finally, every family who has ever trusted us with their loved one's story: you taught me that every goodbye deserves dignity, a touch of laughter, and a whole lot of love.

Thank you for letting me tell this one.

— Martin

About the Author

Martin Thompson is a second-generation funeral director, storyteller, and lifelong Fort Worth Texan. For more than five decades, he has helped families celebrate lives with equal parts reverence, compassion, and—when appropriate—laughter. He believes that honoring a life well lived sometimes requires solemnity, sometimes humor, and always heart.

Martin owns and operates Thompson's Harveson & Cole Funeral Home and Martin Thompson & Son Funeral Home alongside his son, Jon, continuing a family legacy of service that spans more than a century.

When he isn't helping families or writing, Martin can usually be found on the golf course, watching TCU Horned Frogs football, or relaxing at home with his wife, Janice, their family, and an ever-growing pack of loyal dogs, some of whom insist they understand everything he says.

The Mulligan Chronicles: Talking Dog $20, A Texas Tale is his second book, following Funeral Begins with Fun. An edited companion volume, The Mulligan Chronicles: Second Chances — A Story of Loss, Faith, and Redemption, will be released later. He is also the author of Heart and Humanity, a storyteller's history of funeral service, and is currently at work on The Greatest Week in Golf, a love letter to Augusta National and The Masters Tournament.

Martin believes every good story—especially one involving a talking dog—is proof that God still works through humor, grace, and the occasional wagging tail.

www.ingramcontent.com/pod-product-compliance
Lightning Source LLC
LaVergne TN
LVHW020418070526
838199LV00055B/3651